Teyanna Tales

TABITHA C.

© 2024 Teyanna Tales

Printed in the United States of America.

All rights reserved.

TABLE OF CONTENTS

1. Meet Teyanna	1
2. She Thinks She's Grown	21
3. She Fell In Love With The Bad Guy	32
4. New Life	69
5. Self-Awareness	87
6. New Type	104
7. Never Put All Your Eggs In One Basket	118
8. Change Is Coming	130
9. Release It All	153
10. Be Still & Listen	161
11. Beauty In The Struggle	172
12. Power	192
13. About The Author	214

ONE

Meet Teyanna

Just like that; my life changed in the blink of an eye. I knew then that it would never be the same. I'm not kidding! I began an entirely new, everyday lifestyle. Just imagine going from being the Life of the party, breaking necks left to right, showing out every time you show up, to not showing up at all, not seeing anyone regularly, days, weeks, and sometimes months.

How about going from a spontaneous life to a predictable one? Only because it is expected for you to do the exact routine daily. Things became very stressful and highly overwhelming for me. I wanted to give up. But the power of manifestation took the wheel.

I know you're probably frowning and squinting. Probably thinking, "Wait, what? What happened? I'm so confused". Let me rewind a bit and tell you a story. A story that's going to blow your mind. One that I hope contributes a positive effect to your well-being and provides the encouragement you need to keep going.

My name is Teyanna, but everyone calls me Tee. I'm from a little bit of everywhere. I was originally born in Jamaica but raised in the United States. Before my parents split up as a kid, we traveled the world consistently. It was bittersweet. I enjoyed meeting new people, but I hated leaving my close friends behind. My dad was in and out of our lives. Most of the time, it was just me, my mom, and my older brother.

My dad drove trucks, so he spent a lot of time on the road. When he wasn't on the road, he was "still on the road," if you know what I mean. It caused a lot of problems in the house. He and my mom were always arguing about him not being home. Still, as an adult, I cannot understand his way of thinking. His father was never a part of his life. He wouldn't recognize him if he stood right beside him.

You know, most guys whose fathers weren't in their lives growing up want to break that generational curse and make a difference. You also have the others who grow up and become a replica. I mean, he had created a whole family but didn't seem to understand the importance of being a family man.

Sending money here and there apparently wasn't enough for my mom. Legally, they were never married. They lived together, made babies, and paid bills.

He wasn't a bad guy, but he was kind of a bad dad. I mean, picture this, "you never see your old man, so he misses out on many important things in your life. But when you do see him, he shows genuine love and gives you money." What are we, side chicks?

I was a good kid. I mean, I pretty much did whatever my mom asked me to do. I'd always follow her rules, and I'd never disrespect her. Most kids would call her strict, mean, and crazy! At times, I'd agree, but deep down, I knew she was just trying to protect us.

As I got older, things changed. We'll talk about that a little further down the line. Let's go back to my dad. I don't know exactly what happened, but I remember my mom waking me and my brother up in the middle of the night. My dad was still sleeping. "Shhh, be quiet, put your shoes on, and grab these bags." "Let's go," she said. "What the hell is going on?" is what I wanted to say. But instead, I did what she asked.

She already had things in the car outside. It was dark outside, a little chilly and wet from the rain earlier that night. Once we were packed and loaded, she took off. I was so sleepy. While sitting in the back, I leaned my head against the window, balled up under my blanket, and fell back asleep. After a few hours, I woke up. The sun was slowly rising. It was beautiful! It reminded me it was time for a new beginning and gave me a glimpse of hope.

As I looked around, I realized we were on the highway headed north. We had left Florida! "Ma, where are we going?" I asked. "To your auntie's house," she answered. Granted, I had about five different aunties, but I knew who she was talking about. We headed to my mom's older sister's house in Atlanta. She was my favorite of the crew. She was so kind and loving. She never passed judgment and would give you her last if needed.

We used to stay there when we came to town to visit. But this time, we were staying for good. It was the summer ending of my junior year in high school. My last year of school, and here I am, switching states and schools again. I told you it's always something, and we were always traveling. Starting school in Atlanta was different. The people were welcoming but not intentionally. It's like they were all just outspoken. They'd say, "What's up, you the new girl?" "Why are you looking lost?" "I ain't ever seen you around here; what's your name?" and "What's up?" when you make eye contact.

It was so weird; they just naturally started speaking to you. After some time, I made my presence known. I was never considered shy, although I was always considered "the new girl." Once you acknowledge my presence, I'll converse with you. I became very popular. I hung out with everybody. Jocks, nerds, the bougie girls, and the hood ones. My energy was like a magnet; it just naturally attracted people. Which sometimes can be a gift and a curse; you have to be careful who you let in.

I was always invited to parties and always went to different kickbacks with my friends. My mom was still strict but lenient enough to allow me out of the house. I grew an attachment to this city. When it came down to guys, I'd always require them to take me out. Most of them were spoiled by rich parents with good jobs, so they drove nice cars. I didn't have a car. We lived on the same street as the school, so I had to walk if I couldn't catch a ride. But that wasn't often. Every now and then, I'd go over to a friend or a guy's house after school only because there were too many people at mine.

I started coming in late and sometimes not at all. I'd call my mom and let her know I'm staying over a friend's. I began to feel myself. I had a date pretty much every other weekend.

Guys were obsessed, but they knew they weren't getting my goodies. No, I wasn't a virgin. But that was none of their business. High school here was everything I had imagined. I didn't play sports, but I was always at a game. I used to love standing up in the bleachers at the pep rallies, twerking. Yes, twerking at school. I was the life of the party. "Go Tee, Go Tee, Go Tee," they'd yell. All eyes on me, the life!

Toward the end of the year, everyone met with the counselors about college. I didn't know exactly what I wanted to do. I always thought I should be doing something with TV personality. So, I decided to study broadcasting. I passed all my finals and was cleared to walk for graduation. It was such an emotional day. I was so happy and so proud of myself for finishing school. But it hurt my heart that my dad wasn't there to see me. I asked my mom where he was; she said, "he couldn't make it." How could you miss something like this? How could you not arrange your schedule to make it? How could you not know that your only daughter was graduating this year? Even if my mom didn't invite him, he should still reach out to invite himself. I hated him. I couldn't believe it!

    After high school, I worked part-time at a pizza shop while trying to go to school. Notice I said, "tried". Things didn't seem to work out in my favor because I couldn't balance my presence and my future. I was so caught up in what was going on at the moment I overlooked planning ahead. Reports and projects were due in a few days. Instead of working on it, I was at a kickback.

Payments were due for my tuition, but I was behind only because I spent the money on clothes and trips during spring break.

Eventually, I was placed on academic probation. Because my grades weren't exactly what they should've been. My priorities weren't either. I had gotten so caught up in guys and partying with friends that I began to lose sight of myself. I had no idea who the young woman was that I was becoming. I ended up quitting school. I couldn't take it. I became overwhelmed with trying to balance my personal life and education.

I couldn't keep up with the payments, and I couldn't handle the pressure of knowing I would fail. That wasn't like me; I'm a smart girl. I gave up and decided just to work full-time. I worked a lot; I worked overtime and would even go in on my off days. I had finally saved up enough money to get myself a car. I bought a small, cute red Jeep. The perfect vehicle for a young beauty like myself. I got it from a rich older couple. They said it was their granddaughter's, but she had moved to Nevada for a job. She ended up getting something much fancier.

Once I had got my car, my family didn't see me too often. I had no reason to ask for rides. Once I got off work, I'd usually crash at my boyfriend's house. His name was Albert. He and I went to high school together. I called him Ali, like the boxer. But everyone else called him Al. Ali was brought up somewhat similar to the way I was. He never met his dad, raised by a single mom, the only boy out of four kids; his mom didn't have much money but took care of them. You get the picture.

Only his mom wasn't as strict as mine. He didn't have a cell phone in school, so she couldn't necessarily blow his phone up looking for him. Instead, she'd see him whenever he got home. She didn't mind him having company over either; she'd just say, "Y'all better not be in there being grown," while smoking her cigarettes. We kept the door open from time to time. But, of course, the door ended up closed.

I felt like I could be myself around Al. I didn't feel like I had to go above and beyond the way I did when I went out with the spoiled rich guys. It was different. He accepted my natural hair, the chipped polish on my hands, and everything else. He was so funny, and I love to laugh. We'd sit around and crack jokes about people all day. I loved our bond.

Albert and his best friend ended up getting an apartment together. It was in the hood. Nothing I was used to, but I knew as long as I was with him, I was good. Eventually, I became comfortable. I spent a lot of time over there. So much that I was practically living there. I'd go home about two days out of the week. Working full-time at the pizza shop became stressful for me. I worked there for a little over two years. I started to think I was missing out on life. I didn't have one.

All I'd do was go to work, go to Ali's, or go home. Go to work, then Ali's or back home. I liked the money, but I didn't like putting in the work to get it. I ended up resigning, which is probably one of the worst decisions I could've ever made. It seemed like that decision had triggered my life to fall apart. Everything started going downhill.

My mom and I weren't seeing eye to eye. At the time, I felt like she was babying me. Because I didn't have a job, I was at the house more often. Being at the house meant I had to follow her rules. I hated it! I was almost twenty-one, and I figured I should be able to do what I wanted; I was grown. It had gotten so bad between us that she ended up putting me out. I couldn't let her see me sweat. I had my own car; I packed my things and left without looking back. Deep down, I'm thinking, "Where am I supposed to go?" Ali's? Oh no, by this time, he and I had gone our separate ways. This man had cheated on me and gotten another girl pregnant. While I was out working hard, he was working on other women. It still hurts my heart to this day. He still says it was an accident, but this situation, to me, isn't a mistake. We all know the risk of having unprotected sex. This isn't a mistake that can be undone. There was nothing I could do about it. I was done with him.

    I had absolutely nowhere to go. All of my friends either still lived with their parents or went away to college. I drove for hours, crying and crying. "Ma doesn't love me; no one cares about me. My life is over," I said to myself. I had seventy-five dollars left to my name. I was so caught up in "living" that not one time did I think about "saving." I drove and drove. I drove even further until I was tired. I was about 3 hours away from the area where we lived. I had no clue where I was, but I was exhausted and wanted to rest.

I found a decent hotel. It wasn't anything like what I was used to on trips with my friends. But I had no other options and was broke. Once settled in my room, I took my clothes off and hopped in the shower. I began to break down. "Lord, help me! Please, God, it's me. Send your spirit, Lord, please help me", I yelled. I began to hyperventilate while the scorching hot water came down my face and body. I couldn't see; I closed my eyes and sat down on the floor of the shower while it was still running.

"Who am I? What have I done?" I thought to myself. I did the best I could to calm down. I sat there a little longer, allowing the water to splash my hair while I sat and held on to my knees. I then stood up, cleaned my face, and got out. I began to dry off, put my clothes on, and fell to the floor. I knew then it was time to pray. We were a praying family. We may not have gone to church every Sunday while growing up, but I knew enough to call on the name of Jesus. That's for sure! I began to pray, begging God to make a way for me and tell me what I needed to do.

    I felt a little better after letting it all out. I got in the bed and started scrolling on social media. I started chatting with an older cousin in Cali. His name was Fred. Fred has his own accounting company; he was always good with money. I don't know how, but he's always been good with numbers and always had nice things. He was so cool! I told him what I was going through. He suggested I stay with him and his family for a while.

I couldn't believe it! Just like that, with no hesitation. "Why don't you come out here with us for a while, Tee?". I will never forget those words. I looked at the ceiling. My eyes started getting watery, and my heart started racing. At that moment, I knew it was nobody BUT GOD! "Thank you, Jesus, Thank you, Jesus, Thank you, Jesus!" I said out loud. I asked if he could book the first flight out.

The following day, I called my older brother. I used my last twenty bucks to get him a ride to my room. I asked him to get my car and take me to the airport. It was an emotional ride. My brother wasn't anything like me. He was very reserved, laid back, and respectful. He didn't bother anyone, but he wasn't a pushover either. Whenever my mom and I would argue, he'd shake his head and walk away. He never got involved, never tried to break it up, and he never stood up for himself towards her. Instead, he'd talk smack whenever it was just the two of us together. He was very happy for me. He mentioned how he thought this experience would be good for me. Of course, he told my mom I was leaving. She sent well wishes and prayers.

TWO
She Thinks She's Grown

I bet you think I lived happily ever after, and things started to work out for me, right? Not at all. The overall stay was crazy. It wasn't even Fred's fault. I remember one day, we all went to dinner as a family. It was Fred, his wife, two children and in-laws. The weather was warm. It was a beautiful day in the city. While we were waiting to be seated, I remember staring out the window towards the parking lot. I wondered, "Who is driving that Benz Truck, and what do they do?"

I guess I didn't blend in with the family too well because the hostess said, "Ma'am, how many are with your party?" I didn't answer immediately. Because honestly, I didn't think she was talking to me. Did you not see me, a Black girl with long braids, come inside? With this black man, white woman, and mixed kids?! I was so confused. I looked at my cousin. He glanced at me. We both had the same bewildered look on our faces and started laughing.

"She's with us, ma'am," said Fred. You're probably thinking it was a white lady, right? Absolutely not! She was just as brown as me. She looked so embarrassed. She apologized over and over while Fred and I continued laughing. While we laughed, his wife and in-laws had slight smirks on their faces. Of course, they didn't understand the humor behind it all. That's not all, though; I'm telling you, this was quite the experience. Once we were seated, I looked over the menu and ordered the same thing I ordered at all restaurants: pasta. I ordered shrimp and chicken pasta with water. Pasta is my favorite food, and it's not too pricey. It was about $16.99.

The next day, Fred said he had to go into the office. The kids were at school, which left just me and his wife. I was sitting on the couch, going through my phone. She was standing in the kitchen, pouring herself a cup of juice, and she began to question me. Just to get to know me better, I guess. The conversation was fine until she brought up the dinner. She said, "You know, you should be more mindful of what you order when you go to dinner, especially if you're being treated." I just stared at her.

In my head, I'm thinking, "Girl, it wasn't even $20.00. You have on Gucci house shoes! Are you crazy?!" I wanted to snap. But I couldn't react because I had no money, no say so, and nowhere to go. I politely smiled and went back to my phone. Once she walked off, I went back upstairs to my guest room. A few days later, I overheard her and Fred arguing. I knew it was about me because all I could hear was, "Well, she, she, she." Who else could "she" be?

I knew then that my time was up. I went out back to sit on the balcony. It was dark. I propped my feet up on the ottoman and stared at the stars. Fred came and joined me. He didn't say anything at first. He didn't have to. I could feel his energy and could tell that he felt really bad. Of course, the conversation led to me having to leave. Later that night, he booked me a flight back to Atlanta and gave me a little pocket change for the inconvenience. The next day, I caught a ride to the airport. That's when I met Summer, my driver.

After hugging and thanking Fred, I said goodbye. Summer invited me to sit in the front seat. Usually, I'd probably decline the offer because I'd think it was weird. But she looked young like me, and she was pretty. "Ahh, what the heck, why not?" I thought. I'm really glad I did though because we immediately clicked. Based on my body language, she could tell I had a lot going on. Once, she asked me, "Are you okay?" It's like word vomit just came up. I began telling her my life story within ten minutes.

After venting to her, she said she was somewhat in a similar situation. Lucky her, she was getting a consistent unemployment check and driving on the side. But guess what? She was looking for a roommate! She was new to the city and had no family in Cali. I immediately accepted the invite; then I called Fred.

"Cuz, you said you put insurance on my ticket, right? So, I don't have to leave tonight, do I?" I asked. He laughed, then asked, "What are you trying to do, Tee?" I gave him the rundown. Then he asked, "Are you sure you want to do this?" I felt like this was my only option, so I went along with it. Thankfully, he had given me some pocket money. Three hundred, to be exact. I gave it all to her upfront.

Once again, I could feel the presence of God. I knew he was with me, but I'd get discouraged at times and let my mind wander. My mother was a praying woman. I didn't understand when I was younger, but things always worked out for us. For the first few months, things went well between Summer and me. I found a job at a call center. Summer would always be sure to drop me off on time. It wasn't too far from our place. So, I'd just walk home on nights when she'd be driving late. Maybe fifteen to twenty minutes. But in the car, it was faster.

I met a lot of cool people. Very bougie but nice and welcoming. I even met a guy. His name was Darren. Guess where Darren was from? Atlanta! Crazy, right? What a coincidence. He was just in town for work. I didn't understand exactly what he did, but he looked important. Only young like me. Early twenties, tall, with a beard, smooth brown skin, a fade, with a suit and tie. Did I mention the beard? Oh, my goodness, he was so handsome. But overall, a lovely guy.

He said he'd be in town for about a month, which turned into two. We spent a lot of time together. He was so funny! It's like I was some type of celebrity or similar to him. He worshiped the ground I walked on. I wasn't used to this. Anything I wanted, anything I needed, he'd see that it got done. I do everything for myself. Even when I was with Albert, I still had to provide. I mean, I'm somewhat like a bum at this point. How'd someone like me get the attention of a nice guy like this? "He's just being a man and having fun," I thought.

After a while, Summer became unreliable. She stopped taking me to work, and when she did, there was always some type of hostility, which led to me being late multiple times. I had gotten so many points that they ended up terminating me. I needed that job. I was just slowly getting back on my feet. I tried searching for something new, but it wasn't an easy task. Summer and I got into a huge fight because her new boyfriend convinced her I should pay more than I was.

Who takes that type of advice from someone they barely even know? He didn't even stay with us! She knew my situation; I didn't have a job, and this was all her fault. How am I supposed to come up with more money on top of what I usually owe? I told her I was moving out by the end of the following week. This girl had gone insane. She held my mail hostage! Important documents, I needed that stuff! She refused to give it to me until I gave her more money.

    I couldn't argue with her anymore; I didn't have the strength. It wasn't in me to physically harm her because I couldn't afford to go to jail. The situation had gotten so bad that the police had to get involved. Of course, she surrendered my belongings, and I packed up to leave. I called Darren and asked him to take me to his hotel. I needed to calm down and think. Different thoughts were going through my head. I felt like the devil was riding me and trying to bring me down.

Back-to-back, back-to-back. Over and over, I couldn't win for losing.

Darren suggested I go back home to Atlanta with him. He was leaving in two days. It sounded good, but where was I supposed to go? I hadn't spoken to my mom in months. I can't just show up at the doorsteps. At least that's what I thought. He told me I could stay with him. For a little while, just until I got back on my feet. That was the best thing I had heard in a long time. By the weekend, we were on the first flight out.

THREE
She Fell in Love with the Bad Guy

Darren and I never put a title on our relationship. We weren't together, but at times, you'd think we were. But we didn't refer to each other as "boyfriend and girlfriend." He never made me feel uncomfortable while living with him. We didn't have sex, we didn't kiss, and we didn't shower together. Sometimes, we'd cuddle on the couch while watching TV. We'd cook together, work out, and relax on the balcony.

He supported me financially and emotionally and kept me encouraged.

He placed me in the right hands to build my credit. I never understood the importance of it until I began to see all the things he did. It's almost like he could buy whatever he wanted and was living comfortably. But he taught me that good credit will allow you to live this way. I wanted a life similar to his. I had finally got in touch with my mom. She and my brother had moved in together. No one still hadn't heard from my dad after all these years.

    I went to visit my mom one afternoon. She hugged me so tight, like it was the last time she'd ever get to. I could feel the love, especially when her tear dropped onto my cheek. Things got better between us. We developed an understanding. I just couldn't live under the same roof as her. It was for the best.

One night, Darren and I went out for drinks. On my way to the restroom, I bumped into a guy. It was Albert. OMG, this man had grown up; he was FINE!!! I didn't let him know that, though. I politely said, "Oh, what's up?". He and I ended up exchanging numbers. I didn't see an issue with that. Darren and I had an understanding of where we stood with each other. At least, that's what it seemed.

I mean, I'd see him texting other girls here and there. But we weren't together, so what could I say? Al began to blow my phone up! Always texting me, trying to explain his self about messing up. Wishfully thinking things could've been different for us. I think his son was about two or three years old by this time. He explained that he and the baby's mother weren't together; they were cordial and had no drama. I didn't believe any of that mess, but I did remain his friend.

After some time, I completed a training program that trained me in all areas and helped me find a job. I had gotten a job at a small TV station. I worked hard and saved the majority of my paychecks. I saved up enough money to get a place of my own. My first apartment!!! Boy, was I happy. Darren never told me I had to leave, but I felt it was only right that I did. I was so excited about getting my own place that I had no shame in sleeping on the floor. It wasn't even furnished. I was just proud to say that I did it.

I was determined to succeed. I continued to work hard and bring in lots of money. I had gotten two raises within six months. This was a good job, and they had great benefits. I even became an employee of the month. I kept in contact with Darren. We'd speak every now and then. But I consistently spoke to Al. He and I became much closer and more intimate. We became sexually active again, almost every other day.

  I'd have a lot of fun with Al. But it wasn't what I was used to. All we'd do was go to clubs and get drunk. We never went on a real date or did anything similar. I never really felt comfortable telling Al about my dreams and the goals I had set. Because whenever I'd ask him about his goals, he had absolutely nothing to say. He'd say things like, "I know I want a big house, a big family, and a lot of money." "Okay, sir, sounds good, but how are you going to achieve that? What is your plan of action? What goals have you set?" I thought.

You know, I guess it is still considered a date. Even if I'm the one always paying. I didn't mind, though; I loved Al. But eventually, I got tired. Once I stopped paying, it's like we stopped going. Sometimes, we would stop to get take-out from restaurants. Every now and then, he'd contribute to that. But how can you contribute if you're not consistently getting money?

Al and I were very similar in many ways. We were both what you call "go-getters ." See, I didn't mind working hard towards my dreams. I believe that it will all pay off soon enough. Albert, on the other hand, wanted that fast money. He was impatient; he'd do whatever he needed to do to make some quick cash, even if it wasn't legal.

Instead of clocking in at a job, he decided to do tattoos. Don't get me wrong, there are some talented tattoo artists, and some are very wealthy. But doing two to three tatts a week at people's homes isn't enough. I don't know what it was, but it was something about this man I could not shake. It's like, deep down, I was turned off. I was annoyed and fed up with this immature, mediocre relationship.

But I ignored all of those emotions. He was handsome, he was tough, and fun to be around, and, of course, the sex was amazing! I was addicted to him. Looking back, I just sit and shake my head. I didn't realize what a fool I was making of myself. He had pretty much moved in with me. He had trash bags full of clothes all over the place. He'd be gone all hours of the night and come back when he was ready.

One night, I had gotten out of the shower and dived into the bed. I worked a double shift; my body was exhausted. I was scheduled for a late shift the next day, which meant I'd get to sleep in. Al hadn't been home in almost 48 hours. I didn't care; I just wanted to rest. I kid you not. Ten minutes later, I was in a deep sleep. My phone scared me from the vibration. I jumped up. I looked at the screen but didn't recognize the number, so I declined.

Five minutes later, it vibrated again. "Who is this calling me this time of night?!" I thought. I answered, "You have a pre-paid call from...an inmate at", the recording said. "Oh my gosh, he's in jail," I said to myself. Here I am, thinking he's out messing around again or upset because I expressed my feelings about how I want more out of this relationship/friendship; whatever it was that we had, I expected more. But in actuality, the boy had been incarcerated.

He explained that he'd gotten pulled over with some friends. When they ran his name, he had a warrant for his arrest. Apparently, that had something to do with being in the wrong place at the wrong time and missing a court date. He's definitely innocent, based on what he explained to me. But he had no bond.

A few days later, I surprised him with a visit. It was in a small town, about 40 minutes from my place. Nothing fancy, but a little middle-class area. It was obvious I had no idea where I was going. The officer at the desk was very helpful. She greeted me with a smile and complimented my cardigan that matched my headband as soon as she saw me. I gave her my ID and told her who I was there to see. I could tell what she was thinking by the way she started "sizing me up" after looking at Albert's picture on the screen. "What are you doing here visiting a guy like this?" That is probably what she wanted to say. Her smile slowly began to fade away.

When I walked through the door, I saw that tall, chocolate, skinny man standing behind that glass in an orange jumpsuit. My heart immediately lit up. It began racing; I was so excited. I missed him so much. We spoke for about thirty minutes. He explained what was going on and how he thought he'd be getting out before the end of the week or sooner if he makes bond. Eventually, they gave him an amount. He didn't ask me for any money, so I assumed everything was already in process.

He also went on about how he will do better, how much he loves me, and how his love for me is incomparable to anyone else. He went on and on. I believed him. I believed every word. We then said our goodbyes, and he mentioned he'd call when he got a chance.

While walking down the hill to the car, I noticed a girl walking up. She looked out of breath, but she was a little big in the stomach area.

All I could think was, "More power to you, big girl. This hill ain't no joke". She was staring at me until we got closer. I looked at her and frowned. I was confused. Why was she looking at me like she knew me? "Hey, did you just visit someone?" she asked. "Mmm hmm," I said. "Was it Albert?" she asked. My eyes got super big. I paused for a second, then said, "Um, who are you"? "I'm his girlfriend, Alissa," she answered.

"I recognized you from social media. I catch him stalking a particular girl's profile almost every day. I wanted to know who she was. So, I pulled up the profile on my own phone and saw your pictures. You're the girl," she said to me. If only I could explain the look I had on my face. My heart was beating so fast, I kept my cool.

"So, you said every day? I didn't know he had a girlfriend. He never mentioned you before", I said to her. She said they had practically been living together, and she was carrying his baby. I could've screamed; I thought I was about to explode from the inside out. I smiled and denied the fact that he and I had anything going on. Instead, I told her we were just friends and nothing more.

I went back to the car, and I started screaming. "OMG, you've got to be kidding me"! I couldn't believe it. I just sat in this man's face, smiling for over thirty minutes, listening to him sell me dreams, all while he had another baby on the way. How could I be so stupid?! How did this even occur? He doesn't even have a relationship with his firstborn. Was he trying to redo it? I had no idea what I had gotten myself into.

I began driving back home, but I just couldn't stay focused. My eyes began to water, and my head was spinning. I was still in a state of shock; I had to pull over. I called my close friend. Her name was Nyema, but I called her Ny. We met at work and have become closer than ever since. Ny pretty much told me not to get involved; she mentioned this was my opportunity to escape. But I didn't understand; I was already involved. At least, my feelings were it was too late.

Albert ended up calling me the very next day. Of course, he denied their relationship and living with her. But he didn't deny the pregnancy. "I was just messing around; it meant nothing. I asked her to take the pill, but she didn't listen. I swear", he said to me. "That may very much be true, but that doesn't cancel the fact that there's another human that will soon come into this world that you created," I replied.

This man had lost his mind. If a rolling stone was an individual person, he'd be it. I was so confused. Who told him it was okay to tell that girl what to do with her baby? The one that's growing in her stomach. Take the pill? Who did he think he was? God? He has no say so in that. I'm curious: what if she had taken it? Would he have ever told me?

He got released a few days later, and he called me around 3 am asking if I could come get him. You know I went. Looking back, I wish I never answered the phone. I brought him to my house, then got back in the bed. He jumped straight in the shower. As I balled up in the dark, I laid there staring at the light shining underneath the bathroom door. I couldn't stop thinking about the situation. I thought to myself, "Lord, if I'm not supposed to be doing this, please send me a sign." Not realizing this was the sign!

I was in love, dangerously in love. I overlooked all the red flags. I didn't understand how the girl said he was living with her because he had clothes everywhere over here. He had lost his apartment with his friend a while ago. He was so nonchalant about it; I bet it wasn't even in his name. What a jerk, so ungrateful.

    Weeks had gone by; we were actually getting along. I never really brought up the baby situation. I just couldn't handle it; I'd rather not even discuss it. I refused to believe the man I loved had begun to create a family with someone else. This meant there was a permanent attachment between him and another girl. I'd just prefer to face the reality when the day came. Until then, spare me the torture.

    Al had left to do a few tattoos at a friend's house. I just wanted to relax, so I stayed home in the bed. I got on social media and checked my inbox. There was a message from a girl. It was the baby mama! "I know Albert is over there with you. You need to tell him to come get his stuff. Tell him not to worry about his child," the message read. My eyes got big. I turned my head to the side. Again, I was confused and became extremely irritated. Why is she writing me?! How did she even find me?

    I waited until Al got back. As usual, he was nonchalant and laughed. I don't like the way he called himself handling the situation, but I still never responded to her. It was about 4 am. I needed to use the bathroom. I sat on the toilet with my phone; I couldn't go back to sleep. I finally got back in the bed and got on the internet. Immediately, a notification comes from a direct message. It was her! I started to think this girl had some type of tracker on my profile. Why was she even up?

"You dead wrong for messing with him. Knowing he has a baby on the way. By the way, everything he has, I bought him. He has nothing to offer you. You're so dumb!" the message read. At this point, I'm ready to fight. Because who does she think she is calling me out my name and trying to judge me? I couldn't fight a pregnant lady, which made me even more upset. I had way too much to lose. Once again, I didn't respond. I politely blocked her.

I just didn't understand how Al could be so calm about the situation. It's like he didn't care about my feelings. I tried to give him the benefit of the doubt. Maybe he didn't know how to show he cared. All he'd say was, "Just ignore her". Obviously, ignoring her wasn't really working; this was serious. After a time, I guess you can say Al and I were "going steady." I have no idea what to call it. It's like we lived together, but we were roommates in a one-bedroom apartment. I went to work and did my own thing. He went wherever and did his thing.

    I had gotten in contact with Darren. We talked every now and then. We were still really good friends. He wasn't in a relationship, but he'd vent to me about different girls he'd been talking to, and sometimes I'd vent to him about Al. I didn't like to discuss Al too much because it would lead to the baby situation. Deep down, I still wasn't okay. He'd always say things like, "Teyanna, just leave him alone" or "he's not the one for you." Honestly, I was embarrassed. I'd always keep it short and simple when it came down to him. I'd say things like, "I don't know what we're doing. I'm just going with the flow".

Truth is, I knew exactly what was going on. I was taking care of a grown man. I was feeding him, housing him, and providing for him. Hell, I should be called mama. I know mine wouldn't be too happy if she knew about the disgraceful decisions I'd been making. At the time, she and I were on good terms, but we didn't see each other often. She'd probably prefer me to be with a guy like Darren instead. But he and I were just good friends. At least, that's the way I looked at it.

I knew he had some type of feelings for me, but he never expressed it. We were just so cool. It was always such a good vibe with him. We could talk for hours about anything. What I admired the most about Darren was his ambition. He was determined to succeed and worked very hard. He had a plan for exactly what he wanted and exactly how to get there. Darren would give me feedback, ideas, and advice when I spoke to him about starting my own business one day. If only I had listened.

But Darren also never made a move. I mean, he wasn't gay or anything. He was a gentleman. But even gentlemen eventually take the step, don't they? I just assumed he wanted nothing more than good conversations and a shoulder to lean on when he got played by one of those easy girls he had found.

I became very stagnant. I had become comfortable with the way I was living. Go to work, sometimes Ny's house, and then back home. That was my everyday routine. Don't get me wrong, I still had fun and stepped out. When I did, I'd always show out. I was always the life of the party. It could be dead, not too packed. It didn't matter to me. You would always catch me in my own world dancing, followed by a crowd surrounding me. I'd have all types of guys buying me and my girl's drinks. We'd be in VIP. One older guy even sent a dozen roses to a section for me.

From the outside looking in, you'd think I was living my best life and had it going on. However, on the inside, I was just looking for ways to occupy my time to avoid reality. I'm really going through it. Months had gone by. One day, while at work, the receptionist called for me on the walkie. She said I had a phone call. I picked up the line,

"This is Teyanna," I said. "Oh, so you do work here," a voice replied. "WHAT!" I said. Immediately, I recognized the voice. Yep, you already know it was the baby mama! "What Albert got going on? He needs to be ready because it's almost time, and my baby is coming", she said. I politely hung up the phone.

 I told my manager I had a family emergency and needed to leave. I drove home so fast that I can't even remember if I stopped at any stop signs. I opened the door; Al was on the couch playing the video game. "How does she know where I work?" I yelled. He looked so lost and seemed very shocked to hear me speak like that. I continued yelling and fussing. I felt so violated. He picked up the phone to call and confront her. He told her to leave me out of whatever they had going on. He disrespected her pretty badly, but that's what I wanted. She deserved it at the time. In the moment I was impressed, I was happy he did it.

I just couldn't seem to understand why she felt a need to harass me. Why me?! What am I, the therapist? She was lying as well about the baby coming soon. She was only about 6-7 months along. She exaggerated the whole thing. I guess after a while, Al began to feel guilty about everything. He should've. This was all his fault. He started acting super nice toward me for weeks. Random "I love you" texts, jumping in the shower with me, playing love songs, consistently expressing his feelings, and the sex! Oh yes, the sex was amazing.

He really boosted my ego. I began to feel like no matter the circumstance,

I'd always be the leading lady. He said no one else could compare. One morning, after a night out, we made love. It wasn't anything I was used to; it was like never before. Would you believe me if I told you we had gotten into a serious altercation the night before? We went out with a few friends from high school to celebrate our classmate's new nightclub opening. Al was sloppy drunk already while we were on the way. He had been taking shots by himself while I was driving. He snuck the bottle inside and kept drinking. Straight white, no chaser.

I couldn't tell you where his mind was because he had obviously lost it. He began speaking to me crazy. He spoke as if I thought I was better than him, then started degrading me. He even mentioned the baby situation. He told me to mind my business. Who did he think he was? Why was he talking to me like this? Was he holding this in the whole time? You know, they say the truth comes out when a person is drunk.

People were staring at us. He kept walking up in my face, and then I'd push him away. He never hit me, but he did snatch me by my arms. I was so embarrassed. I could've busted him in the head with one of the pool sticks on the table. I didn't want him to go back home with me. I didn't even tell him I was leaving. He must've noticed me walking outside, then came running after me. He was literally running! The car ride was completely silent on the way back to my place. That's because he was passed out in the passenger's seat against the window.

Once we got to the apartment, he threw up in the parking lot. "Clown," I mumbled, then walked inside. I immediately went to the shower; I locked the door while I was in there. I cried and cried and cried some more. I cried until I just couldn't, until I felt sick to my stomach. I was done with him. This man had embarrassed me, disrespected me, and insulted me. I had never felt so low in my life. What was in it for me anyway? Why was I even still holding on? It wasn't even worth it. I told myself when he sobered up the next day, he had to leave. That was my word!

When I got out of the shower, I saw him sleeping on the couch. I went to get in the bed. The next day, that's when it happened. I slept great! I had a few drinks the previous night, so I was slumped. The sun woke me up. Where my bedroom window was located, the sun was shining directly in. I just laid there, thanking God for another day. As I lay there, balled up under my blanket, Al came into the room. I don't know if he was trying not to laugh at my facial expression, but he had a smirk on his face. "You still mad at me"? He asked. I didn't answer; I just rolled my eyes and grabbed my phone. "You gone let me make it up? I had too much to drink; I'm sorry, Tee," he said.

I don't think there was any way to make up for that type of behavior. He really did what you call "showed his true colors." Then, he grabbed the bottom of the blanket near my feet, put it over his head, and crawled up. Slowly making his way to the top. A tingle went through my body, as he penetrated me. I was in pleasure overload. Then suddenly, I felt his release!

"What are you doing?" I yelled as I pushed him off of me. I jumped up and ran to the bathroom. I sat on the toilet for a second, praying everything would shoot back out, and then I got in the shower. "OMG, OMG, OMG, OMG" was all I could think in my head while bathing. I just knew he didn't do what I thought he did. "He can't, he couldn't have", I thought. I said I was done; this was supposed to be the last of us. We couldn't seem to get along, but we couldn't stop having sex. How does that even sound?

A few hours later, he got a phone call. He stepped outside and sat on the steps. The steps were right by my window. I could hear everything. He was on the phone arguing with another female. Turns out, it was the baby mama. Can someone explain to me where it's okay to argue with another woman while at your woman's house? Actually, when is it necessary to argue with someone who isn't your girlfriend/boyfriend anyway? He sounded like their relationship mattered to him, and I'm not talking about a co-parenting relationship. How is this even possible? We just finished having sex a few hours ago.

    I still wasn't completely comfortable with the baby situation; I was still hurt. But I was learning to tolerate it. Only, this wasn't a baby discussion. He must've enjoyed arguing because when he came back inside, we got into an argument. It was bad. It was so bad it led to him grabbing my neck and slamming my head into the wall. He then called a ride and left with his trash bags of clothes. Time had gone by, I hadn't seen or heard anything from Al in almost a month. It felt good not having Al around. I just did my own thing, and I liked it. I began to catch up with an old guy friend named Ryan.

    I met him while I was in training when I first moved back to Atlanta. We went on dates here and there. But as usual, I'd end up talking back to Albert. Ryan and I were close work friends until he transferred to Florida. He and his friends decided to throw a birthday bash for his cousin in Miami over the weekend. They invited me and a few friends to come visit. I didn't have many friends anymore, only because we had all grown apart. I spent a lot of time at work, so I took Ny, of course.

It was actually the weekend before my birthday. It was so much fun! We went bar hopping, to the beach, to clubs, and to a nice dinner. I laughed so much during that trip, and it felt so good. I remember it like it was yesterday. I'll tell you what didn't feel good, though. The cramps that warned me that my cycle was coming. I remember praying it didn't come while out of town. I wanted to enjoy myself. After a long night out, Ryan woke up early the next morning. He went to get us breakfast. I was exhausted and still sleeping in his bed while everyone else was awake and talking in the living room. I'll never forget how comfortable that low, king-sized bed felt.

"Girl, you gone sleep all day? Come eat", he said to me. It seemed like those were some powerful words he had spoken. As soon as he left the room, my phone rang. It was Albert. He must've seen the pictures we posted on the internet because he was so determined to find out what I was doing. Again, we argued. He was very disrespectful. Who did he think he was questioning me and then comparing me to another woman? We shared our differences, and I told him I never wanted to see or hear from him again.

    I couldn't let Ryan know that I was at his house, crying over another guy. I told him my stomach was bothering me and that I needed to just lie down. Weeks had gone by. My stomach was still cramping, and I was consistently running to the restroom, especially at work. Standing up all day made me feel pressure, like I was about to pee on myself every ten minutes. I could tell that my cycle was coming, though. It hurt so bad, but it was taking so long! My co-workers kept encouraging me to take a pregnancy test. I just refused to believe that I was pregnant. The pain I was feeling felt something like a bad UTI or a menstrual cycle. I knew it was coming soon.

    The end of the month had come, and I still hadn't seen a drop of blood. I finally worked up my courage and bought a pregnancy test. I sat on the toilet while waiting for the results. It was blurry. I saw faint lines, but it looked like two of them. My eyes began to water, and I wanted to cry. All I could think was, "I said I was done with him. Please, God, don't let this be true. NO! I don't want anything to do with him anymore. Please don't let this be true." I waited a few hours, and then I took another test. This one said negative; it had only one line. I was so confused.

I went ahead and called the doctor to schedule an appointment. I needed accurate results. The next morning, I video-chatted with Albert. I didn't think he would answer, but he did. How do you think he responded when I told him I may be pregnant? "Welp, it's not mine," he said. "Are you going to take the pill?" Nope, nothing similar to that. He was smiling. I didn't crack a smile. I was confused. What was he smiling about? Did he plan this or something?

A few days later, the doctor confirmed that I was five weeks and six days pregnant. I was in denial until I saw a little peanut on the screen and then heard that rhythmic heartbeat. It brought tears to my eyes. I'd never heard another heartbeat beating so close to me before. This one was growing inside. "Lord, what am I about to do with a baby?" I thought. Time had gone by, and Albert was still not back in my house. One night, around 3 or 4 am, I was awakened out of my sleep. My phone rang. I didn't recognize the number, so I declined the call. Three minutes later, it rang again. I'm in the first trimester of my pregnancy, so you know I am exhausted, and all I want to do is sleep. Any unnecessary disturbances pissed me off! "Who is calling me?" I said.

I answered. "You have a pre-paid call from an inmate at..." the recording said. "Oh my gosh, are you kidding me?" I thought to myself. It was Albert, he was in jail. He and I still weren't on speaking terms, and I had no idea what he had going on. My mind went racing.

All I could think about was how much I didn't want to go through a pregnancy all alone. I could only imagine how the other girl felt. She was much further along than me. Apparently, whatever he had gotten himself into, he was going to be gone for a long time.

FOUR
New Life

About 2-3 months had gone by. I remember driving throughout the night, crying and praying that God would release him. This was my first baby. "I need him", I thought to myself. I did not want to go through this alone. Darren reached out to check on me. I did tell him that I may be pregnant, but I never followed back up to confirm. Once I delivered the news, he asked me, "How do you feel?" I felt angry, embarrassed, and, most of all, huge! He offered to take me to lunch, and I was craving pizza. We went to a pizza spot near my house. The waitress came over and said, "You guys make such a beautiful couple; I know that's going to be a precious baby." We laughed, and he answered, "Oh no, I'm not the dad." I just put my head down and kept eating.

  Darren and I caught up for about an hour or two. He told me he had gotten into a relationship. But they weren't on the best of terms at the moment. Darren is such a good guy. Why the heck is he out with me if he has a girlfriend? I guess it didn't matter; they weren't speaking, and there was nothing he and I could do together but eat. I began to open up. By this time, Albert had been released from jail. We still weren't on good terms either. He had moved in with a friend and their family. He hardly ever called to check on me. He never came to any appointments or asked if I needed anything. We never even discussed baby names. I could tell

Darren felt bad for me, but once he puts his mind on something, he's all in. At this point in life, his focus was on his new relationship. I wasn't necessarily jealous, but Darren would've made this experience much smoother.

    I stood up at work all day, every day. My feet began to hurt so badly, which led to my back. One day, I decided to reach out to Al about my feet; they had swelled up. He was pretty nonchalant about it. He said, we're not together, so why should he have to rub my feet? He had gotten to a point where he didn't even seem concerned. He wasn't supportive of anything throughout the entire pregnancy. I can count on one hand how many times he had actually rubbed my stomach. You know, him rubbing and speaking to my stomach would've been good for the baby because Al's voice would be recognizable. Everything about this experience was horrible. Albert didn't seem to care about me or his unborn child. He didn't care about anyone but himself.

Albert received a letter in the mail about a court date. He called and asked me to take him; THE NERVE! Of course, I took him and looking back; I wish I never did. Do you know this man cursed me out in the lobby of the courthouse? We got into it because I was encouraging him to find a real job and explaining that things were about to change for the both of us. He needs to do better. He felt offended and began to disrespect me. I threatened to leave him, but he said he didn't care, so I did. Yep, I left him downtown at the courthouse with no way back to our side of town. It was like a 35-40 min drive. As I wobbled down the sidewalk and headed back to my car, I just kept thinking, "Why doesn't he respect me? Why isn't he taking into consideration that I'm carrying his child?" You know they say, "What the mother feels, the baby feels as well." All my baby could feel was screaming, yelling, high blood pressure, anger, and sadness over and over.

  The gender reveal was about a day or two after the courthouse brawl. I had previously given Albert the information, so I told myself I wouldn't call to remind him. Of course, he didn't show up. But called a few days later, trying to play the victim. He said it was my fault for not calling that he wasn't there. I didn't even call to tell him the gender. I posted it on social media. The blue crazy string was being sprayed all over me in the street by my friends and family. I fell to the ground. It's a BOY! It was a baby boy. All my life, I had wanted a son as my first child. God had already confirmed in dreams that I was bringing a son into this world. I dreamed about women delivering boys, blue confetti, anything blue, you name it, I saw it. But I was in denial because I just knew God was giving Albert a daughter.

The further along I got, the more excited I became to meet my baby. I had already convinced myself it was only going to be the two of us. The closer it got to the end, the angrier I got towards Al. I called to ask him if he had a few dollars to get the food for the baby shower, "Na, I don't," he responded. Just like that, not even "When do you need it by?" or "I don't right now, but I'll see what I can do," Nonchalant as usual.

I thank God for my mother and my paycheck. We did what we had to do to get everything we needed. It was beautiful, jungle-themed! For the first time throughout my entire pregnancy, I was happy. I was surrounded by love. We received so many gifts that it looked like I could go about 3-4 months before I needed to come out of pocket. Everything that I needed I had received. Albert just sat there smiling as if he played a part in anything. I barely spoke to him at the baby shower; I was mingling and allowing that positive energy to pour into me.

    Not too long after the shower, I explained to Albert that I needed him to stay with me. It was getting closer and closer to my due date, and I wanted everything to be perfect. I imagined going into labor in the middle of the night while the two of us were sleeping, then he rushed me to the Emergency room, and then the baby arrived. Nothing wrong with that; that's usually how it goes, right? Yea, not on this end. Of course, we can't seem to get along; Albert's mind wasn't on the baby coming; it was more focused on making a small piece of change from doing tatts and driving around in my car.

WHAT was I thinking?! What is this? WHO DOES THIS? A lost woman, that's who. I had lost myself. I did everything I could to accommodate this man, to try and please him, but in return, I only got cheated on, disrespected, a text/call every now and then, no emotional support, no financial support, or enough sense to sit down and discuss the future of the life were creating. But I loved him; at least, that was my excuse. "I have to stick with him; I can't be looked at as another one of his baby's mamas." Because he and I had so much history, I just knew things would be better with us.

Another night, another argument. I had no idea the type of pain I was causing my baby. Not necessarily physical pain, but the type of emotional environment I put him in. Remember, babies feel exactly what the mom feels. If she's stressed out all the time, always yelling, angry, or sad, that's what they'll feel. The same goes for happy, relaxed, and healthy moms as well. Just think about it: those "cry babies" and busybodies during your pregnancy, weren't you always on the go? Did you experience a lot of anger and yelling? How about the ones who meditated, ate a lot, and went with the flow? You've got a little chill one, don't ya? I'm no scientist; I'm just speaking from research and experienced moms' feedback.

    Al asked me to drop him off at a friend's house and decided to stay there instead. I had previously gone to the doctor. They told me if I didn't have my son within the next five days, they would induce me. It was day 2 out of 5 that day, so I packed everything and went to my mom's. I refused to believe that they were going to have to force him out. I knew he was coming, so I needed to be ready. By being ready, I meant someone who could rush me to the emergency room when it was time. We had a good time over my mom's. She had her own place; she'd been there for almost a year now. She was working and back on her feet. From the outside looking in, mama was paid! She did have a degree, though. Things weren't going well for her when we first came to Georgia, so it was really good to see her doing well. She cooked me whatever I craved, and we laughed and danced, laughed and danced all night until she got tired. I kept dancing; I felt so free.

Within that moment, nothing mattered. Not the fact that I hadn't had any emotional, financial, or physical support for the past nine months, not that my vagina felt like it was about to explode due to the pressure on my uterus, not even the fact that no one was downstairs dancing with me. I was happy; I was relieved. I knew then that he was coming very soon. I dozed off on the couch while watching TV. I was woken up by a sudden sharp pain. It led me to have to use the restroom. As I sat on the toilet, the sharp pain came again. It was like my menstrual cycle, but worse. I began to breathe really fast; my heart began racing. "OMG, what's happening?" "Too much dancing," I thought to myself. I noticed when I got up that my mucus plug had popped. I didn't think anything of it, and the pain had gone away.

I turned off all the lights and went upstairs to bed. About 2 hours later, I went back to the restroom. The pain started coming back. I began to tense up, and I fell to the floor. I balled up and tried to catch my breath. I didn't have the strength to stand. It seemed like as long as I stayed balled up, the pain wouldn't come. I crawled back into the room. Approximately 20-30 minutes later, the pain came again. "OH, ok, it must be time," I said. I screamed for my mom to come in. She ran so fast across the hall. "He's coming," I yelled. She was dressed and ready within 5 minutes. We had already packed the car up, so when the time came, we could just go. We were out! About half a mile out, the gas light came on. "Are you kidding me?" I said. This morning couldn't get any worse, and we had to stop for gas. My mom drove that car as if she was a police officer with lights and sirens going. She even ran a few lights. By the grace of God, we didn't get caught.

  Once we arrived at the hospital, they checked my cervix and determined that I was only about 3 centimeters dilated. I had to be at least 10. I was pissed; I had never felt this type of pain before. I wouldn't wish this pain on anyone. Eventually, I was somewhat relieved after the medication kicked in.

After sitting around waiting for over six hours, it was time! I was so numb from the epidural they had given me that I felt absolutely nothing. Not even the midwife's hands inside to measure. I was able to look in the mirror they gave my mom to hold while I was pushing. I'd never seen anything like it before. A tiny human, being pulled out of this no longer tiny hole. The way the hole stretched so wide to allow him to come was just unbelievable; I couldn't believe it!

  His eyes were open, and then he began to cry. They handed him to me, and I began to cry as well. I looked at him, then looked up. "Thank you, God, Thank you, God, for my son." I have a son, and I did it! What a beautiful blessing he is, I thought to myself as I lay in the bed while they cleaned him off, etc. I began to think, this man isn't even here. I wondered if he would've been as supportive as my mom was if he had been. I wonder if he would have been ready to tear that hospital up when my blood pressure dropped and I began to turn grey in the face. Would he have encouraged me to keep pushing and made me feel comfortable? It was pretty sad because he was a free man. Meaning he wasn't incarcerated or anything to keep him from seeing his son, whom he had created, come into this world.

My baby and I stayed at my mom's once we left the hospital. We stayed for about two weeks; looking back, I wish we had stayed longer. I was so paranoid; I couldn't help but consistently walk over to the bassinet to see if he was ok throughout the night. "Is he breathing? Is he ok"? I kept thinking.

My mom was very helpful. I had to get stitches after being cut open during the delivery, so I was very sore for a while. I had never been in that type of position for so long. My muscles were so weakened I could barely walk, let alone pick up my baby. We went home after a few weeks, hoping Al would come to stay to help out for a while. What was I thinking? Two months had gone by, and I hadn't heard a word from this man. No video chat, no how's he doing, do you need anything, nothing!

If anyone ever asks me for advice on having a baby, my first question would be, "Do you enjoy sleeping"? If so, don't have kids. He woke up every two hours to eat or be changed. Repeatedly, for months, he'd wake up around the same time. I began to get the hang of this thing called motherhood. Carrying his car seat up two flights of stairs every day, leaving him strapped in on the floor while I ran back and forth to the car to bring in groceries, mastered feeding him in my arms while eating dinner by myself, and even learned to hold him while cooking dinner sometimes. Months had gone by; I became numb to no support. I was used to showering while he was locked in the bathroom with me in his swing. Sometimes, he'd scream/cry so long and so loud, which led me to take a shorter shower; sometimes, I wouldn't even be able to shower at all because I couldn't calm him down and became so tired that we both fell asleep. We definitely grew an attachment for one another, and he was always with me. Everywhere I went: the store, dinner with my girls, doctor's appointments, you name it. I still believe my mom loved him, but she was not dependable when it came to babysitting. I had never experienced real "me time." My brother had moved away and gotten married; we see him every now and then, and my aunt had gotten older and not the most reliable. It was just me and him, and he was a mama's boy for sure.

FIVE
Self-Awareness

A year had gone by. I had gotten promoted; my son was walking, sleeping through the night, and had more money and fewer problems! Of course, I was still single, but at this point, it was by choice. It was kind of hard at first to date due to not being so flexible with my schedule and limited sitter issues.

The raise allowed me to pay for a sitter when needed, but not all the time. It was just enough to get by. However, at this point in life, dating was different for me. I wasn't just looking for someone to take me out and spend money. I wanted a family; I wanted someone who was ready to accept me for me and someone to love and accept my son. It was hard; not many guys even acknowledged the fact that I had a child. I would never force him on anyone; that's not like me. But he was a part of me now. There weren't many "Hey, how's your son doing," it was more "How are you," "Wyd," and "When am I going to see you." Boy, bye!

They didn't understand that I was a single parent who didn't have much support. Never mind the fact that I can't just call his dad to say, "Hey, can you get him this weekend?". Whenever my mom agreed to keep him, she'd asked for the exact date and time in advance. These grown boys didn't know what they wanted. It was a waste of time. If I wanted to have some real fun, the girls would have to come over, or we'd find a "kid-friendly" environment to visit.

I was ok with being alone. I had become addicted to myself and my own thoughts. Thoughts about what will happen, and gratitude for what was actually happening. I was healthy, my son was healthy, I had a job, and we had our own place and a vehicle. I was blessed! I didn't need a man around to prove that to me.

The older my son got, the more challenging it had become for me on my own. It was time to start potty training, learning words, and practicing discipline. He began to develop his own personality, which became quite a struggle. I remember being extremely tired from working 12 hours and coming home to bathe, feed, and get him ready for bed. I had dozed off while reading to him, and when I woke up, he was finally asleep, too. I was so thankful, laid him in his bed, and crashed. Can you believe he was up within 5 hours?! I was pissed!

But what could I do? If I stayed asleep, who knows what he'd get into, and if I got up, I was going to be cranky because of the amount of sleep I had gotten. It led to me being cranky; I tried to give him a snack and dozed off. I woke up; marker drawings were all over the walls. This is the part when I wish we had a roommate, a partner, or someone, anyone to help. I just wanted to rest. I had worked six days straight. Granted, he probably missed his mom, and he was hungry or needed to be changed. But Mama was tired!

Things had changed; I couldn't strap him in the swing to relax anymore while I tried to soak in the tub. Now, he'd pull his pants down to climb in with me. He wanted to play with the bubbles and go "swimming." He wanted to splash, and he wanted to be up under his mom. Again, mama was tired!

I couldn't even eat a bowl of cereal. There was no such thing as "me time" in my home. I had given him the last slice of pizza we had from the night before. So, I ended up fixing a bowl of cereal for myself. He had eaten the pizza, saw me eating, and then attempted to climb up my lap to taste the cereal. I wanted to throw the bowl at the wall. But instead, I took a deep breath and gave it to him. At that moment, I knew I was reaching my breaking point. I went to my room, closed the door and screamed! Screamed so loud my throat began to itch, causing me to cough and hyperventilate. I cried and cried. I cried some more. I cried until I just couldn't breathe. As I caught my breath, I began to think.

Was all of this built up from within? Was this necessary? Did I really just spazz over a bowl of cereal? No, it wasn't about the cereal. This was being held inside for a long time. This was built-up stress from not being alone, not resting, not being able to think or have a moment to myself, except in the middle of the night while he was asleep. This was from trying to read and do research after putting him to bed. Then he cried and threw tantrums because he wanted to be under me, but I wanted space. This was from no one helping financially with childcare or pull-ups and clothes/shoes. It was from sitting up in the emergency room multiple times and urgent care all night right after getting home from work by myself. This was having to take him inside every store with me because he couldn't stay at home or in the car, and he threw tantrums, whining and screaming because I wouldn't carry him while trying to push the grocery cart. This was me, tired. I had crashed mentally. This was my breaking point.

I began to slack in nearly everything. My mind just wasn't all the way in. At work, I was the personal assistant and protégé of the Head Director, Missy, short for Mysoure' like the state. Everything she did, I assisted. Whatever she needed, I did. I was the best to ever do it if I do say so myself. She meant business, and she did not play. She was very professional and punctual, but she also was a shoulder to lean on during hard times. She'd always mention to me how I reminded her so much of herself. She was also a single mom; she had a daughter about six years older than my son. She was engaged to her boyfriend and co-parented with her daughter's dad.

Missy became very attentive to me and noticed that my attendance had begun to slack, I was forgetting to complete important tasks, and my attitude wasn't that approachable. I didn't notice any of this. I was just doing what I like to call "taking it a day at a time." I was annoyed here and there, but that's because people are dumb. People consistently asked questions that they should know the answer to or didn't seem to know how to utilize their resources. OMG, like, let me breathe.

A colleague approached me while making coffee and said "Tee what's going on today"? "Another day, another dollar," I said. "Naw, like, what's going on with your hair? I'm not used to seeing you like this," she said. "You're that comfortable around me that you think you can judge me?" I asked. She then apologized and stated that my hair usually has a particular style each day. This time, it was more like a wash-and-go. I didn't see anything wrong with it. Who cares? No one there was checking for me anyway.

Truth is, she was right. Granted, she could've come up with a different approach. However, I did look different. My hair was all over the place. It was a thick, pretty texture, but the messy bun was beyond messy. I didn't feel like putting a lot of effort into baby hairs or curly sideburns. Nor did I care that my nails were overdue for a fill-in or that I'd worn the same cardigan three times that week as if it was a work jacket or matched every outfit.

    My skin was developing acne, and my legs were a bit hairy. I had completely lost myself. Mentally, I was exhausted. I had no life, and I was not taking care of myself as much as I should have. My routine was to wake up, get myself and my baby ready, drop him off, go to work, get off work, pick him up, and go home. We'd bathe, eat, sometimes I'd eat while I worked, try to watch TV but have to fight with a toddler on laying down while the light from the television shined, and end up turning off the TV and going to sleep. On the next day, we'd wake up and repeat. On off days, we'd sleep in a little; I'd cook breakfast, clean up, and maybe work or sleep while he messed up the house again. This was an everyday routine. For months, this went on, leading up to an entire year.

During my quarterly one-on-one meeting with Missy, she went over my strengths and opportunities. She then followed up on my behavior over the past few months. She had brought to my attention that I was showing signs of postpartum depression. It was nearly two years since I had my baby. I didn't even know it could last that long. My emotions had gotten the best of me; I had lost my confidence, and I became lonely, angry, and just not myself.

It sucked pretty bad because I had not noticed it. Recognizing it first plays a huge factor. That way, you can get the right assistance needed immediately. Sometimes, if you wait too late, depression can cause a lot of issues through finances, wardrobe, and just your overall well-being. I began to look back at the times I yelled and became angry over the tiniest things my son did. He's a baby, and he was just doing what babies do. But I was angry, I wasn't happy, I was tired, and I needed a break. I had no one. No one seemed to understand me; it was always, "That's what we go through as moms; you'll be fine. Don't mistreat him; you need to calm down." It was never, "Tee, how are you feeling? Is there anything you need? Would you like for me to help with this or that?".

You know what they say, though: closed mouths don't get fed. I also never expressed to my family what I was going through and how much I needed them. I wanted to, but I just didn't think they'd understand or want to keep him unless I was working. Missy had gotten me in contact with a local therapist who charged a little to nothing. She was so kind. She listened, she asked, and she helped. She gave me homework assignments, taught me best practices, and dug deep into me. I also dug into myself. She helped me learn myself.

That's right, learn myself, the new me. Once you create life in this world, you become a mother. You will never be the same girl you were prior. Your life will never be the same. For some, it can change for the better; for some, not so much. I do hope that, in the end, it works out for the best. I began to practice morning meditation and recite my daily affirmations aloud.

Every morning, before I started my day, I would sit on the floor and begin to stretch. I started with my legs, gripping my toes and forcing my chin to touch my shin. I then would sit with my legs crossed and stretch one arm across my chest while holding it with the other, then push my elbow towards my back. After stretching, I then sat quietly, with my legs crossed and palms upward on my thighs, ready to receive whatever God had for me.

      I began to breathe, slowly in and out. I then began to pray. Regardless of my current situation, I gave thanks. For another day, for my sanity, for my son, my home, my job. Although it wasn't much, although he drives me crazy, although it's hard, I was thankful. I was thankful because it could've been worse. "I am beautiful, what I wear on my head or back does not define me," "I am financially stable, money is not an issue for me," and "I am healed, I am healthy, everything attached to me will win," I repeated, over and over.

I continued to go to therapy once a week. After a time, it led to every other week. I had also joined a mom group. It was created by another single mother, an African American from Philly. We would video chat once a week, listening to a guest speaker while practicing exercises and worksheets similar to meditation. About 98% of the other women on the call were single moms. I had no idea this had become a "thing." So many moms with different-aged kids raise them on their own with little to no support from their fathers. The sessions were very therapeutic and sometimes a little emotional.

I'm thankful for the tribe I encountered. Never had I met so many individuals who stuck together and genuinely wanted to help one another without wanting something in exchange. They gave away clothes, shoes, toys, money, tips and tricks, resources, open gems, and more. They were moms; they made it happen by any means. I was paired with a young lady who also lived in Atlanta as my MOM partner. We were each other's help.

    Alice was her name. She and I immediately clicked. We just had so much in common. She was pregnant with her second child but was also a single mom with a son. Alice had a good job and provided for herself with the help of her mom sometimes. When she needed a break, I'd babysit. When I needed a break, it was her turn. Sometimes, we sat at each other's house together for hours while the boys played and mingled. We could talk about anything. We cared so much for each other that we felt obligated to help with whatever we could. She was awesome, and our bond was unbreakable. Still, to this day, we're friends. I am truly thankful for her.

SIX

New Type

Another year had gone by, another birthday without Albert. You haven't heard that name in a while now, huh? Yeah, I forgot about him too. He had become non-existent. I had finally gotten to the part of my life where I didn't care if he was involved or not. It was no longer an emotional topic, and I had forgiven him without even getting an apology. Mentally, I was healing. I began to enjoy the mother-son bond we had together more than ever. We slowly began to understand one another as I took my time with him.

    I picked up hobbies instead of sleeping during the time my baby was at daycare. I enjoyed painting. I felt so free, sitting on my balcony facing the tall, dark trees, listening to the wind blow and the cars drive by. Whatever my wrist did, I let it be. When I wasn't painting, I was walking. I walked a few miles a week around the neighborhood to increase my vitamin D and develop some type of workout plan. I wanted to lose my baby weight so bad, but I just was not that dedicated to running.

After a while, I felt like myself again. I had cut my hair, not too short but in a blunt, blonde bob. I also bought a new wardrobe and moved into a nicer neighborhood. A new construction townhome in the city. Everything felt as if it was what needed to be. I was happy and healthy, had gotten a raise, prayed more, and was feeling myself again. I mean, I really feel myself. Posting a selfie every other day and posing in nearly every mirror.

I made a deal with my mom to keep my son for one weekend a month, Friday through Sunday afternoon. I had to bribe her with money, but I didn't care; I just wanted a break. I didn't always do anything, but it was an opportunity to have time to myself. I was able to clean, sleep, watch TV, or even soak in the bath without any interruptions. Alice had delivered the baby, and I still helped whenever I could, but I remembered how stressful it was for me on my own with a newborn. I wouldn't dare ask her to babysit along with her other son. That's ridiculous. My raise had come just in time, just enough to pay my mom.

I found a new hangout spot in the city, an art museum. I heard about it through a co-worker. He told me he and his wife went, and they served free cocktails if you purchased a ticket. I began to go twice a month. I couldn't afford any of the paintings for sale, but just to take a selfie or ask a stranger to catch a particular angle was a pleasure. I had become someone I never knew. What joy would I have gotten years ago at a museum? I had always loved art, but not so much to stare at images that a non-artist would think is just a simple circle. Not realizing it's more than just a circle. The colors tell a story through their pattern within the image that starts through the diameter.

    I learned that concept from my new friend, Joe, short for Joell. I met Joell one evening at the museum. As usual, I was trying to take a photo of myself standing in front of the newest artwork in the gallery. This time, I had set a timer and propped the phone up against the wall. I had about two glasses of champagne by then, so there wasn't a shy bone in my body at the moment. I didn't care who was watching from afar. I was killing it! I was getting good shots! At least until this guy walked right in front of me as soon as the flash went off.

Gasp. "Ohhhh dang, I'm so sorry. I swear I didn't see your phone right there," he said to me. "Really"? "Everybody else saw me." "You think I'm just standing here posing just for fun?" I responded. He laughed and said he was looking straight forward, headed to the restroom. He didn't notice me or the phone. He just so happened to hear the click and see a flash. He insisted on taking a photo of me to make it up. I told him I thought I had got some good ones on my own. Really, I was becoming shy and didn't want to pose in front of a camera for him. He was handsome, and I just couldn't.

After we looked over the photos that I had taken myself, it was obvious that I had been struggling and needed a photographer at the moment. I did want a good picture in front of that particular canvas. "What the heck," I thought, "it's just a picture; go on, girl." He looked over the pictures with me to see if he needed to take more. We laughed and narrowed it down to the best two. "You look so free," he said to me. "What?" I said while laughing, trying not to seem confused. "You look so happy like you don't have a care in the world. It's something about your glow; it looks good on you", he said.

I didn't know what to say. I smiled and tried to keep my composure. In reality, I wanted to say, "What glow, I've been through the mud and back." Instead, I said, "Thank you, it wasn't always like this. You have no idea". He went on to say how interested he was to hear more about it. But that was not a story I wished to tell. I changed the subject and asked if he still needed to use the restroom; it's been at least fifteen minutes. He laughed and asked me to wait for him. We sat and talked for about twenty to thirty more minutes. Just laughing and discussing how we both had come alone, literally just to get out of the house and view some nice artwork.

    Who does this? Was this a thing? If so, I've been missing out. Fine, brown-skinned guys go to museums and meet girls? He was tall, with a low fade, nails were fairly clean, and very well dressed in casual short-sleeved button-ups, nice pants, and shoes. I almost forgot; he had a beard. JACKPOT!!! You know, I love beards. He was a contractor/handyman. He had his own business and worked as a third-party agent to repair homes. He spoke a little hood, but that might've been that Atlanta slang. It didn't matter, I liked it. He almost reminded me of Darren. Except he was a bit more laid back. Darren was such a good guy, but I never mentioned he was flashy. He was not intentionally flashy, but he would always have on an expensive designer regardless of whether it was lounge-around clothes or if he was going out. Joe didn't look to have on any type of expensive designer, but I could tell he wasn't broke. I could tell just from conversing. Just within a few minutes, I could see he was about his business and was a go-getter.

As we wrapped up the conversation, we exchanged numbers. He asked if I minded if he called me versus text. I explained that I preferred text because I'm a mother. My son may want my attention at the moment, and I don't want to be stingy with either of their time. So, it's best to text me and allow me an opportunity to tend to my child and text back as soon as I can. I could tell from his facial expression that he wasn't used to hearing that type of response. But I wanted to be honest and set the standards upfront; I have to tend to my son. Unless you're ready for the chaos, it's best to text and take it slow. He smiled and said, "I can respect that;

at least you're honest. I like that, Teyanna".

After some time, it became an everyday routine for Joe and I to speak. Whoever woke up first would send a good morning text. When my son was sleeping, I'd call, or if I was driving and kid-free at the moment, I'd call. We spoke a lot. He'd even be on the phone with me while he was working sometimes.

We started hanging out periodically. He was very patient with me. I never invited him over to my house. Instead, we'd go on dates to different restaurants, museums, and even picnics. He often asked about my son and how things were going. This was after a time when I began to open up about my experience as a single mother. Things were going really well for us;

even after all this time, we still had not put a title on our relationship. Were we in a relationship? I didn't know.

Life has its tricks and mysterious ways. Things were going well with me and Joe. Then, out of nowhere, Darren reached out. He knew nothing about another guy; he just simply reached out. I still loved me some him. Darren was one of the best friends a person could ask for. So sincere and just solid. Meaning, he was authentic and didn't let small things come between the ones he genuinely cared about. It's always a pleasure speaking to him.

At this point in life, Darren had resigned from the company he worked for. He started his own marketing company. Don't ask me exactly what he did; I never understood, but it took off immediately. It was something with marketing and helping people with businesses. Darren is smart, and one thing he knows how to do is make some legal money. His birthday was coming up in a week or so. He was throwing a red carpet-themed party. I told you, he was flashy and loved to clean up nice. Indeed, he did. He asked me to be his date. "Me?! The man of the hour's date"? I thought to myself. Once again, he was on bad terms with his girlfriend. They had broken up. I couldn't turn down an opportunity like this.

    Yeah, I wore a few dresses and heels before here and there, but never had I gone to a red-carpet-themed party. I agreed to go and asked a lot of questions about the colors, style, etc. "Don't worry about all that, Tee, you know I got you. We'll go to the mall this weekend to get everything you need", he said. This was like a dream come true; I couldn't believe it. Never have I ever experienced a guy taking me shopping, especially for his own birthday.

I remember going downtown to the luxury stores. He bought my heels and my purse, and we ordered my gown offline. He even bought new sneakers for my son. He always asked about him and followed up on whatever milestone I previously told him about with him. I loved it.

Joe began to reach out, and I always seemed a little too busy for him. It wasn't intentional, and he did nothing wrong. I just missed my friend and was excited about this party. He asked what I was doing the upcoming weekend, and I explained that I would be in attendance at my friend's birthday party. I left out the part where I was the birthday boy's plus-one.

SEVEN
Never Put all Your Eggs into One Basket

My mom agreed to keep my son the night of the party. I just had to come get him before church in the morning. He was a busybody and would not sit still. I watched a few tutorials over the years and mastered my makeup skills. I couldn't afford to pay anyone to do it for me. Instead, I did it on my own. I still had my hair braided from a month ago. I slicked my edges down and styled it with a swoop and updo bun. I looked beautiful. I was so proud of myself.

The party started at eight that evening. Darren picked me up at eight-thirty. He wanted to make a grand entrance. He came inside to use the restroom while I put on my shoes. "Dang, girl," he said while smiling. "You looking gooood," he said. I smiled and thanked him. My heart was racing when we got in the car. I was listening to him on the phone, calling his crew to let them know he was on the way. That meant all eyes were about to be on us.

I don't know why I was so nervous; I was never shy. I was always the life of the party. We pulled up to the front door, and the valet team opened both of our doors. Darren came around and then reached for my hand so we could go inside. I could hear the DJ on the mic saying, "The man of the hour, presenting Mr. Darren James." He sounded like the guy presenting professional boxers. It was hilarious. He was so happy, just cheesing and dapping people up as we walked in. I just kept thinking to myself, "suck it in, girl, suck it in, suck it in." I smiled and focused more on my stomach than anything.

He took me to our seats and then went to mix and mingle. We had a time! The DJ was on point, and Darren brought the crowd! I received so many compliments, and I felt so beautiful. I went to the dance floor a few times to dance a bit. I didn't want to seem like a party pooper staying seated all night. I danced with Darren a few times, a little twerking here and there, but kept it classy, of course. We slow-danced once, too. I wonder what it meant to him, standing there closely against one another, dancing to "So Into You." What a time! Everything felt so perfect. I never wanted the night to end.

After the party, we went to an after-hours lounge with a few of his friends. We got a section and popped more bottles. We were so lit. All eyes on us. Everyone kept looking over to see who was in that corner section. They probably thought we were celebrities based on what we had on suits, ties, button-up shirts, dresses, and heels. All the girls kept eyeing Darren. I didn't blame them, though; I mean, he looked amazing, with a crispy haircut and trimmed beard, shiny diamond earrings, two gold tennis chains, pinky rings, clean manicured nails, gold cufflinks, with his shirt halfway buttoned up. He had taken off his blazer at this point. His pants were pulled all the way up, none of that sagging showing his boxers; they were fitted just right with his Christian Louboutin loafers.

I don't understand why, throughout the night, I kept questioning how I got so lucky to be by this man's side. Then I snapped back into reality and thought, why not? His attire didn't make him any different from who he was before he put it on. Meaning at the end of the day, this was my friend before all of the spotlight. When I had absolutely nothing, and he was making ends meet, we still had a strong bond.

Darren and I left earlier than everyone else. We were pretty wasted. Once we made it back to my place safely, I suggested he stay due to how far a drive he'd have to make while being under the influence. We crashed on the sofa, laughing and reminiscing about the night. It's never a dull moment with Darren. As usual, we could talk about anything for hours. The conversation took a turn once he began complimenting me again and letting me know that he saw how all the guys were checking me out. "I was so focused on my stomach not poking I didn't even notice them," I said to him. "I like how your stomach pokes; that's nothing to be ashamed of; it's sexy," he responded.

    He then began staring into my eyes and leaned in to kiss me. I kissed him back and began to grab the back of his head to pull him closer to me. I couldn't believe what was about to happen. This is Darren we're talking about; he's never made a move on me before. He began to lay me down while kissing me. My body was tingling. He slowly began kissing every part of my body while rubbing his hand up the split of my dress.

Once he got below my waist, he stopped going any further. I had never felt anything like it before. The longer he was down there, the harder I tried to force his head towards me as if it could come any closer. He then came back up and began to penetrate me. In all my years of living, I had never experienced an orgasm, and here I was. I screamed, not because I was in pain, but because I couldn't hold back the release anymore.

We took a shower and slept the rest of the night. Everything was perfect. I had my alarm set early the next morning; I was so sleepy I did not want to get up. But I knew I would never hear the end of it if I didn't pick my son up in time. Darren got dressed and went home while I got dressed to head to my mom's. On the way over, I received a text, "Good Morning, Beautiful." It was Joe! Oh my gosh, I forgot all about Joe. He began to ask me how the party was and did I enjoy myself. I told him it was very nice and that I had a really good time.

I began to feel bad, like I wasn't being honest with him. But I was, it was nice, and I really did enjoy myself. Except, I left out the other details. But why should I feel bad? It's not like we were in a relationship. I didn't cheat on him. He really liked me, though; it was very obvious. I liked him too, just maybe not as much as he liked me. "What have I gotten myself into?" I thought to myself.

A few weeks had gone by, nearly a month. I had been off and on with Joe. Nothing happened, we just became a little distant from one another. We stopped speaking every day; we spoke maybe every week, but not for long. Darren went ghost on me. I hadn't heard from him since the night of the party. I called him once or twice, but he never answered or returned my calls. I began to question myself, thinking, was it something I did, or did I say something wrong?

It turns out Darren and his ex were back, "a thing." She had posted a picture at dinner with him and then tagged him in it. Because she tagged him in it, I was able to see that that's what had been going on. I could not believe it; my heart dropped; I was so angry! I just kept thinking, "What is it about this girl that caused you to go back after you had recently been with me? Why not communicate and tell me you're back with her? Why would you just leave me hanging like that?" That was one of the most disrespectful things he had ever done before. Of course, I had been through worse with Albert. But that caused me to think that he never actually cared about my feelings. I meant absolutely nothing to him.

I wanted to send a long text message letting him know how I felt, but I had never done anything like that before with Darren. How would that make me look? I just wanted him to know that it did affect me. I wanted him to know that I was beginning to develop strong feelings. I wanted him to know that being with him felt like a void had been filled, but it was now empty again. I just could not do it; I never liked rejection. Ignoring my calls was a sign of rejection, and I did not know how to handle it. With that being said, I was not going to pour out my feelings and not receive a response, I would lose it.

Now, I understand the meaning behind "Never put all your eggs in one basket." I put so much time and energy towards Darren that I completely forgot about Joe. We ended up going our separate ways. I saw him on a date from a post he shared, and honestly, it didn't even bother me as much. I couldn't blame him. But that could've been me if I had learned to date without such strong intentions. I think once I became sexually active with Darren, my intentions with him changed. I had high hopes that he and I could become a family and grow with one another. In reality, I should've been casually dating, having fun, and then eventually seeing where it goes. Of course, it's never encouraged to date without any intentions at all; that would simply be wasting someone's time. I mean, just take it easy and not put so much thought into it immediately.

EIGHT
Change is Coming

Well, I'm still single. But this time, I'm not mingling. Two years had gone by; I had absolutely no one close enough to even consider being in a relationship with. I left the company I had been working with and branched off to do my own thing. Now, I didn't just quit out of nowhere; I went part-time and then eventually took a leap of faith after I built a strong audience.

I had started my own channel. I started off with a podcast recording only my voice. But I enjoyed being on camera instead. I would speak on motherhood and the struggles of being a single mother. At first, I was just recording just to vent and clear my head. It worked, too, releasing those built-up emotions that often came due to Albert still not being involved and not helping me raise his son. But the girls tuned in! They loved it. I would receive direct messages and comments with questions, advice, and suggested topics for the next episode.

Your girl was booming! I had begun to get booked for women empowerment events to come and speak. I started getting paid for events, and after developing a large number of viewers, I began getting paid for the subscribers. It was so easy because it was all authentic. I was just being myself and speaking my truth. Never had I ever imagined that women would idealize someone like me.

Things begin to work out in my favor. I got back on track with my self-care journey and with my relationship with God. Before I did anything and made any decisions, I spoke to him, I prayed, I meditated, and I became patient. I learned to wait for an answer. I felt so free, I was alone, but I did not feel lonely. I was the only source of income in my home, but I was not financially struggling. It was such a blessing to be doing something I loved and not feel like work.

My son had begun Pre-K, which meant childcare was now free. He made me so proud. I never understood how someone could be willing to miss out on something like this. The whining and baby talk had stopped, the potty training was over, and we were set for success! I loved my life. We traveled together, and fans would tune in to watch our vlogs. We were goals! I had to release all things that were not meant for me back into the atmosphere. I asked God to prepare me for what he had in store for me. I wanted to be ready when it was time. Each night before bed, I would say my prayers. But in my prayers, I included a husband. I learned to become more specific, someone who loved me for me and loved my son as their own.

Someone who I was very much attracted to, who loved and respected their mother, who would support me emotionally, financially, and in every other way. Someone who was ambitious, who prayed to the same God as me, and someone who loved me and my son unconditionally.

I was not following Darren on social media, but I would see him in my list of viewers when I posted things. Not just occasionally; I mean nearly everything I post. I would just smile and ignore him. One day, I decided to look at his page. All the images of him and his girl were deleted. "Hmm," I thought to myself. What is this about?

I still had never got a chance to express myself and tell him how I really felt. I could not seem to get this man off my mind. Even if it was for just a second, he crossed my mind every day. I couldn't let him know that, though. I had to pretend I was unbothered. I'm supposed to be "that girl"; I'm not supposed to be pressed about a guy. I had fallen in love a long time ago and was in denial. I was in, deeply. But I could not push myself to reach out to him.

All these thoughts were going through my head. Then, suddenly, the next day, I received a video chat around 8/9 pm. It was him! "OMG, look how God works," I thought. I answered so unbothered. I didn't show any signs of excitement at all. He stated that he had departed ways with his girlfriend. I didn't believe him. I pretty much told him to stop reaching out if he wasn't completely over her. This isn't the first time they have parted ways. I am no one's rebound, and I was done playing games.

He then told me he would call me back. A whole year had gone by, and he never called again. I still think about him often. But during that time frame, I never lost my focus. Yes, I casually dated. But no one gave me that feeling that I was looking for. I didn't see any type of role model for my son to look up to, and their looks just weren't all that. I was still celibate, and I was okay with that. My career was still successful, and I was still living my best life while trying to be the best mother I could be.

Alice's birthday had come around. She and I kept in touch. She was throwing a party at a club downtown. I missed her so much; I was not going to miss it. My brother and his wife were in town. They agreed to stay at my house for the weekend and babysit so I could go out. It was much easier getting a sitter now at this age than it was when he was smaller.

Alice's party was lit! It was jumping, and the DJ knew exactly what to play. I needed to use the restroom. As

I walked in that direction, I had to pass the bar. Guess who was at the bar? Darren! We immediately made eye contact. He smiled like he had just received the best news of his life. I couldn't resist smiling back, but of course, I had to talk junk along with it. I asked what he was doing there; he said that he stayed in the area. He wanted to get out of the house, so he came to get a drink with his boys.

He then offered to buy me a drink. After I used the restroom, I sat and caught up with him for at least 15-20 min. He was still single. He said he had been focusing on work and trying to stay out of the way. I loved that about him: no drama, no extra baggage, always minding his business and getting to the money. I got so caught up in conversing with him that I almost forgot who I originally came for.

We had caught up on a lot. He asked about my son and how he was doing, motherhood in general, each other's careers, etc. I could talk to him about anything; it was just a natural, easy thing to do. I danced with Alice for a few more minutes, then told her I had to head out. She was having so much fun I don't even think she noticed I was gone. After telling Darren I was about to head out, he insisted on walking me to my car in the parking garage.

We sat in the car and continued talking. This time, I felt the urge to get to the bottom of this back-and-forth nonsense. So, I asked him what it was that caused him to go ghost on me. What exactly did I do? He stated that I didn't do anything. He expressed that he had deep feelings for me that he was unable to control and that he had been in a serious relationship before that didn't work out. So, when he gets the feeling around me, he does what I like to call "run from it." He admitted that he was scared. It kind of makes sense, though, because I had never confirmed any sort of feelings towards him. Who desires the feeling of rejection? I know I don't, which is why I always try to act uninterested. But I did not realize that what I was being was childish and pushing him away. This is just my personal opinion of the situation. Looking back, it probably should've been explained.

We were both pretty faded while having this conversation. I kissed him and told him I didn't want him to feel that way. After I took the initiative, one thing led to another. It was like fireworks going off inside of me. I couldn't resist the urge to say how I felt, "OMG, I love you so much!" He paused in mid-stroke; he stared into my eyes. His eyes were so big and glossy at the moment. He smiled, kissed me, then whispered in my ear, "I love you too, girl." Just a few minutes later, we both released and then departed ways.

During my drive home, I smiled the entire 25-minute ride while blasting my R&B Love songs. I had fallen in love with my best friend. I don't think my night could have gotten any better. The next day, I was in complete mommy mode. I spent the entire day hanging out with my son. Although I cherished the moments we spent together, he was driving me insane. Now, this began over time. The older he got, the more out of hand he became. We had gotten passed the waking up every other hour, the consistent crying because he doesn't understand the "I'm actually making your bottle right now if you'd just be patient with me" concept, and the disappointment in waking up 4-5 days out the week to change wet sheets and scrubbing poop off the floors. Yeah, we had gotten way past that. You see, now, at this point, the tantrums occur, acting out in public, throwing objects, biting, hitting, and his favorite word is now "No."

He was also a busybody; he wasn't like your average toddler. You couldn't take him out in public and let him sit on your neck because he'd try to jump off. You couldn't take him to a baseball game, hoping he'd get excited about the loud yelling, clapping, and fireworks because he'd cry about going up and down the stairs and getting to the field. He loved to get into things, lotion especially. Really, anything that was creamy that allowed him to run his hands together and against furniture, clothes, anything you name it. He didn't sit still while I tried to have dinner with him at the table. Instead, he chose to get up every 30 seconds to run in a circle, grab a toy, spill his food, and then come back. Whew, the list goes on. He was a piece of work. But in reality, he was just being a kid.

So, it's been almost a month since I've seen Darren. I haven't heard from him again either. Here we go again with this going ghost and back to playing games nonsense. I mean, who does he think he is, popping in and out of my life when it's convenient for him or when he feels like it? What's the deal? I did not understand. I video-chatted maybe two times and probably called just once. Video chatting was our thing. We rarely communicated through text or telephone. But he didn't answer! What is it?!

I tried and tried as hard as I could to think of any reason he'd be ignoring me. For the life of me, I couldn't think of anything. I gave up, at least I thought I did. Until I began thinking about him again, all day, all night, and every day, I couldn't see myself with anyone else. I couldn't take anyone else seriously. I couldn't focus on anything or anyone because my mind was always on him and how badly I was hurting. I just didn't think it was fair to come into someone's life, express feelings for them, have sex, and exchange energies, then disappear. You can't do that. If I wasn't as sane as I am, things could've really gone another route. That is dangerous!

I began to notice something was off about me. I had taken a break from social media and vlogging. All I wanted to do was sleep. I took some time off work for nearly a month. Thank God for the funds I had aside to cover rent. During that time, while my son was in daycare, I'd sleep. When he was home with me, I'd sleep. Instead of taking him outside, to the park, or out for fun on the weekends, I'd sleep. He would try to interact with me and wake me up, but I didn't even want to interact with him because I just wanted to sleep. I was very much alert about what he was doing and paid close attention to his well-being, but I still just wanted to lie down.

I know what you're thinking, but that's not it. I had become depressed! I was grieving, my heart was broken, and I didn't know how to fix it. So instead of sucking it up and moving on, I held on tight to my emotions and slept it off. But sleeping didn't really help. It was a temporary thing. Once I woke up, it was back to reality all over again. I declined social gatherings and anything else that required me to be happy and act as if everything was okay. I was not okay, and I had finally realized it. Before I had entirely made up my mind, I said I would try one more time. I mean, why not? He was very much worth it.

It was the holiday season, a little close to Christmas. As much as I would've loved to spend it with him, I knew that wouldn't happen. So, instead, I decided to give him a gift. I wanted to spend money on something, but that wouldn't mean anything. He had money. He had material things. I decided to put a little more thought and love into it. I wrote a poem. Okay, don't laugh. It was really thoughtful and somewhat deep. I wanted to be sure he understood how I really felt.

Let me read it to you:

"When I look at you, I see such a beautiful man
Beautiful does not only apply to women but is also generally pleasing within
Now, don't get me wrong, you look so strong
Actually, you used to be

Back when you used to work out consistently
Back when you used to be sweet on me
I'm talking about heavy
Real heavy
When we were close friends but somewhat going steady
When I had no one else to call on
I knew I could always call on you.
You didn't know at the time, but your conversations always got me through
Those hard times when I didn't want to open up about falling
For the wrong guy and letting him treat me like anything
Yeah, you told me to let him go. But see, I didn't know
that what you were saying was actually true
He was not the one, but it took for me to actually meet you

To demonstrate that type of foundation begins with friendship
Got each other's back
Somewhat like kinship
To see the representation of a hardworking man
One who's going to get it and not have out their hand
Not gone depend on anyone but himself and the man above
Even if someone doesn't do it for you, you still show love
Because you're solid and so sweet
I've always loved how you keep yourself up
Together and so neat
Before, the designer and trendy things before the jewelry, watches, and the rings
When I rode in the Mustang with the top down, I felt so free

Like nothing could touch us just you and me
I felt safe in a different place
But I couldn't shake that negative space
Those dark clouds kept following, and I rode along
Unknowingly that what I needed was right there all along
When I hear a certain song, I think of you. When I hear your name, I smile
When we have sex, it's like, wow
Boy, the chills that go down my back, right before I release, I feel it in my crack
Then you came inside of me
Willingly knowingly
That this is where you want to be
Just like the seed you're trying to create hold on, wait, let me not eliminate
Those times you joked and called my baby your son

I loved hearing those Words
I felt like I had won
But I couldn't let you know
Because suddenly you would go
Missing, you know what you call ghost
I'm not used to that, not from little or from most
I don't do second fiddle
Baby, I'm second to none
I am one of a kind, I'm not doing this for fun
When I tell you I love you, believe me, it is real
I understand you're hesitant and need time to heal
But let me help you understand, and I'll support you if you were my man
Behind closed doors, I'd tell you where you're wrong
But I'll have your back in public, I know how to stand strong

I'll pray with you,
I pray for you already
I ask God to give me clarity because my heart is heavy
My love is patient, my love is kind, it does not envy it's you on my mind
I will nurture you; I will care and encourage you
I want you, my best friend
Let's start a new beginning, but remember
True Love never ends."

It's nice, right? I was so nervous and hesitant about letting him hear. But I felt like I had no choice. Who knows what he thinks is going on in my head right now? He needs to know! I typed it up, sealed it in a red envelope, got a fancy box of chocolate and a bottle of Champagne. I ended up mailing it to his house. I wouldn't expect anyone to respond promptly after reading something like that. I mean, that was a lot. But it's my truth, and I felt a little better after letting it out. I gave him some time, about two weeks to be exact, and still nothing. That was my cue to go ahead and exit. I just knew that he had moved on, and whatever he felt back in the day clearly wasn't the same now.

NINE

Release it All

I begin to go to therapy. But not only for him. I was still somewhat depressed and still having trouble finding myself. Therapy was the best thing I could've done for myself. Being in a safe space with a complete stranger who doesn't judge. Working with someone who actually listens, has patience, and helps me dig until I find myself at the bottom, then picks me back up. Such an amazing experience!

    Now, let's be honest. This didn't happen overnight. It took time to get my "mojo" back. I started off keeping track of my emotions. Every day, I would write on my calendar a number rating from 1 to 10, 10 being the best and 1 being the worst, based on how sad I was feeling. I saw lots and lots of numbers below five at one point. Then we increased to 6, which was manageable, and eventually progressed to 7, then 8. It took for me to really think and dig to determine what it was that I enjoyed doing. What is it that will make me happy? I enjoyed being outside. I used to love being around people, but that required me to interact. While feeling this way, I didn't want to interact with too many others.

After dropping my son off in the mornings, I would walk. I wrapped my stomach up and walked for about 30 minutes each day. In the beginning, I only walked for about 10-15 minutes. As you can see, baby steps were the key, and I gradually increased over time.

Over the weekends, I slept in a little whenever I could, whenever my son didn't come climbing on my back and pulled the covers off of me. Before or after breakfast, depending on my mood, as long as it wasn't too hot, we'd go on the back porch and practice yoga. I wanted to enroll in a class, but that cost money, which I was becoming low on. So, I looked up routines online and followed the steps. It was amazing: breathing in the positive and exhaling the negative. Releasing all the pain, heartbreak, sadness, loneliness, and extra weight. It felt good to just let it all go. Most of all, it felt good seeing that smile and those dimples on my baby boy's face while stretching with his mommy.

    I also started going back to church with my mom, mostly on

Wednesday nights for bible study. The closer I got to God, the more focused I became on Him. The more I learned and meditated on Him, the more things began to work out for me. I began to walk by faith, meaning I consistently reminded myself not to worry about anything because I knew He would provide all my needs. I became more positive. If things didn't go the way I wanted, I looked at it like it wasn't meant to be. Because everything that I need shall be supplied by God, it's like I was shaken back to reality and remembered that he would never leave me nor forsake me.

    He will never put me in a position that he did not think I was capable of handling. He had already written the story; it was all a part of the plan. Here I was praying and hoping that he'd "send help," meaning send someone to assist with this heavy load. But then I had to realize that it wasn't another person that I needed. It was already in me. I just had to pull myself out of that dark place to find the strength that was already within.

I got a part-time job working from home for a marketing company. The position was part-time, but you'd think it was full-time based on the checks. I started off in an entry-level position. It was a great company with great benefits. I didn't even need a degree. They did internal training. I became so good at what I did that within a year; I had worked my way up to a Lead. That position became a bit overwhelming over time. So, I branched off to the training department. I began hosting virtual workshops training employees on various topics. Talking to people and teaching them became something I always had a thing for. I really enjoyed doing it. It didn't even feel like work.

I gradually started the podcast back up. The girls missed me! I think it had been over a whole year since they'd heard anything from me. I spoke my truth, as always. But I wanted to explain to them that it's okay not to be okay. I needed to take some time off, and that's ok. Although I strongly disliked Albert and wished he was around to help with his son. I couldn't give him all the blame. I took full accountability in even pursuing a relationship with him. I knew the type of man and father he already was. What was it about me that would make him do anything differently? Absolutely nothing.

I learned to find my own faults in my actions. Even with Darren, as I was healing. I realized that I was so concerned about not getting hurt that I held back for so long. If I had been honest and upfront about my feelings, it's possible things could have gone another way, even if we didn't end up together. At least the expectations and intentions would've been laid out. It could've been determined then if he actually wanted to be in a relationship with me at all or not.

With my son, I have every right to get upset because, just like any other mom, I'm human and have feelings. However, taking my anger out on him for something he has no control over is below the belt. Getting irate because he wants to climb on me or refuses to listen is not the answer. I could've redirected him in a much calmer tone and mindset. I could've easily walked away and just took a breath to calm down.

But at the end of the day, I was learning. I took it all as a lesson learned. I still give thanks for the experiences. If it never occurred, I would easily fall for the same thing again in the future. If it hadn't happened, I wouldn't be who I am today, sharing my story with others who may have similarities within their personal lives. I learned that when bad things happen, sometimes it brings you closer to God. When situations bring you closer to God, consider it a blessing. I'll elaborate more on that topic later on.

As you can see, life was good. I had my ups and downs, but things were working for my good.

TEN

Be Still and Listen

Life is not predictable. Even if you follow the same plan each day, always remember that tomorrow is a new day, and always expect the unexpected. I say that because never in my years of living had I imagined my life to be what it had become. It started with me having a slight sign of insomnia. I could not go to sleep. This was on a regular basis. Even if it was pitch black and quiet in my house, I would stay up so late, just lying there thinking.

I would have visions. I don't mean daydreaming. I mean clear visions of what the future was holding. Let me elaborate a little. I envisioned myself in a higher position at work, and through the trials and tribulations, I got the promotion. Some individuals didn't think I deserved it, which led to a lot of obstacles I had to overcome. But it was already a part of his plan. I had already seen it.

I envisioned myself standing in a driveway with my baby on my hip. Two years later, I had closed on my four-bedroom home. Aside from becoming a mother, that was one of the hardest processes in my life. The enemy had come from every angle, trying to attack. I had almost given in. There were not enough funds, not good enough credit, paychecks not posting in time;

you name it. Each time I wanted to give up, the Spirit kept showing me that image. "It's already done, it's already done," I would tell myself.

I began going back to Sunday service with my mom. This church was pretty big. They had services for the youth and adults, as well as playtime for the babies. The youth group hosted a program about walking into your purpose. They asked if any adults would like to come and speak. I thought nothing of it. But Miss Katie thought otherwise. Miss Katie was over the youth department, ages 14-20. I met her years ago when we first came to Atlanta. She was like a 2nd mother that I tend to forget I have. She never passed judgment, and before she ever voiced her opinion, she'd always say, "Tell me how I can help." I loved her, she knew almost everything that had gone on with me.

My mom and Miss Katie were both very proud of my transition and all that I had accomplished. Sometimes, I didn't think it was much of a transition; then, I'd look back at how far I had come. I took Miss Katie's advice, joined the program as a panelist, and began to speak. My legs kept shaking, and my heart was racing. Why was I so nervous? Wasn't I used to making video recordings for a living? In the back of my head, I kept thinking, "Someone is going to judge me. They'll never look at me the same; they're going to think so low of me, etc."

But as I listened to my voice come through those speakers going out into the crowd, the attention of those young people that I had. The tears that were shed, the applause that was received, the hugs, and "Thank you, I needed to hear that;" were nothing but God reminding me that "No weapon formed against me shall prosper." The devil wanted me to back down from the opportunity. He didn't want me to encourage the youth to "Trust in the Lord and lean not on your own understanding." He didn't want me to warn them about how he comes in various disguises and doesn't always come as an evil/hideous creature. But as long as we are covered in the armor of God, he can stand no chance against us. He didn't want me to declare victory over each and every one of those children's lives. But God!

During this time of my life, is when I realized it was time for me to stop denying it and walk into my calling. I learned that when God calls you to do something, you can't run from it. You can try to go the other direction if you want. But he will put you through hell and bring you down to your lowest for you to realize that you need to be still, listen, and reroute yourself.

The process of listening and actually hearing what God is trying to tell you to do comes with a lot of sacrifices and a period of isolation. He knows that if you are still in contact with certain individuals, you'll never reach your full potential. He knows that certain individuals mean you no good and are praying for your downfall or will betray you in the near future. He works in mysterious ways; He will break up the best of friends, the closest relatives, and relationships to get you where He wants you to be. Sometimes, nothing bad even happens. You just naturally outgrow each other. But it was all a part of the plan.

God doesn't only use people to get your attention. He also uses your surroundings. Certain things won't feel the same; old things won't excite you anymore. It's his way of moving you. If you try to ignore it, he'll make you more uncomfortable until you realize enough is enough. Albert is the perfect example. God had given me so many signs time after time to let him go. But I ignored all the red flags and continued playing with fire. God had given me a child with a man who was not going to carry his weight by being actively involved. Everything was going to fall on me, and he was not going to make it easy for me. It took for me to carry his seed to realize I wanted nothing else to do with that man. I wanted to give up so many times, but God!

It took for me to be in a season of isolation to see what God was trying to show me, to hear what God was trying to tell me, and to go where God was trying to take me. It took for me to lose everything that I had fallen hard for to realize that was not for me. That's why it didn't work out.

A few weeks had gone by, and I still could not sleep at night. I began listening to my Bible on an app until I fell asleep. The more I listened, the more I learned. The more I learned, the more I wanted to teach others. That's when I begin to ask God during my prayers, "Lord, what is it that you have called me to do?" "Please give me clarity on the next step in my life. Lead me to fulfill my purpose."

I went to bible study on Wednesday. While waiting in the hall for the staff to bring my son, a member approached me. "Hey Teyana, how are you doing this evening?" she asked. "Hey, I'm doing well, thank you," I responded. Then she said, "We're ready when you are baby". I frowned, then smiled. "Ready for what?" I asked. "For you to preach the word, baby girl. You do know that you have a gift, right?" she asked. "Ahh, yes, mam, yes, ma'am, in due time. I got you," I said to her.

Wow, I felt like that was a sign from God. It's like it couldn't get any clearer than that. Here I am all hours of the night studying the word, while it became heavy on my heart to spread it to others, all while asking God to reveal to me what I'm supposed to be doing. That's it; I knew just what to do. I reached out to Miss Katie the next day, asking her what steps I needed to take and how exactly this worked. She then sent me information about enrolling in ministry school.

It took a lot of discipline. But I was dedicated and determined not to let anything get in my way. Not even my son doing cartwheels throughout the house, about to give me a heart attack while I tried to read. I continued working my job, being the best mother I could be, and praying and focusing on myself. Life was good. I was always too busy to hang out with anyone; it's not like many reached out anyway. But I didn't tell anyone what I was working on, not even my mother.

When my last semester of ministry school came, I went to my mom's house. I handed her an envelope with an invitation. "A graduation from what?" she asked. She continued reading, and her eyes began to water. She grabbed me and hugged me so tightly. As she hugged me, she began to sob. "Thank you, Jesus, thank you, Jesus!" she yelled. She then wiped her face while facing me and said, "Minister Teyana, my baby is going to be a minister. Look at what God did. I am so proud of you".

Hearing those words filled my heart so much. I began to cry as well, then hugged her again. "I love you, ma," I whispered to her.

ELEVEN

Beauty in the Struggle

Now, I don't want you to think this was a sudden change. This is the summarization overall. I had to have a meeting with certain members of the church; their approval mattered as well. I didn't just take a course and then begin preaching and take over the church. I was a youth minister, and I studied and memorized Scripture. I prayed for hours, waited for a sign, and took a step of faith.

    I did what I could to keep the community's young adults involved with the word of God. So, I did my research to determine what approaches I should take. Aside from speaking to the ones in church, I also spoke online. Yes, through social media. I had already built a fan base through the podcast show. That was the perfect opportunity.

I consistently posted inspirational, motivational, and transparent posts on my profile. A lot of individuals became drawn to me. I could see all the reposts, tags, etc. It was a confirmation that what I was called to do was working. I can't make these things up; social media is the new networking platform. After a few tags and reposts, my followers increased. As my followers increased, my inbox and emails did, too. I began to receive requests for bookings again. Not necessarily to preach but to tell my story as a motivational speaker.

    This was one of the best things I could have ever done, and it changed my life. One day, I was booked for a huge annual conference in the city. Vendors, speakers, and even celebrities were known to be there. There was such a variety of knowledge being given to the audience. It was amazing. I don't want to exaggerate, but there were well over 500 people at that event. We had multiple stages depending on your specialty and topics discussed; people were everywhere.

    After I had wrapped up my time, I walked off stage to find something to eat. I had taken off my heels and changed into my sandals. That place was huge, and my feet were hurting. As I walked past a particular table, a guy stood up and rushed over to me. He said, "What's wrong, pretty lady? Are your feet hurting?" I turned my head towards him and immediately started laughing. It was Darren! "Is it that obvious?" I asked. I began to ask what he was doing there. He explained that his company was one of the vendors there. I saw his crew with the set up at their booth, passing out flyers and selling merchandise. I wasn't surprised, though; these events are up his alley.

He congratulated me on all my success. He then went on about how he saw my picture on the promo page and was in such high spirits. He mentioned that he was in the crowd listening for a few minutes. I always wondered how I would react if I had ever seen him again after all this time. It had been almost an entire year. But I had changed; I wasn't angry anymore. I was so calm, happy but calm. He asked if I had plans afterward and then mentioned attending dinner to catch up. I accepted the offer and told him to meet me at a particular place by 7:30 pm.

As I was approaching the restaurant, my anxiety started kicking in. My heart was racing, and I began wondering how this night was about to go. I started taking deep breaths, in and out. Whatever is meant to be will be; if it's for me, I won't have to force anything, is what I reminded myself. I got my car valeted and then walked inside. Darren was waiting in the front with two dozen red roses in his hands. I could have cried. My eyes became slightly watery, and I smiled from ear to ear. After thanking him, I asked when he even had time to get them. We literally had just left the arena not too long ago. He said that he had gotten them prior to the event. He was determined to find me at the conference. We were immediately taken to our seats. He then pulled my chair out for me, then took his seat.

"So, I want to go ahead and get straight to the point, Tee," he said. He immediately apologized for ghosting me after all this time. He admitted that he was way overdue for that. He then explained that I did nothing wrong and that it was not my fault. He made a promise to himself to become a particular person, and he knew what he wanted in life. He was determined not to let anything or anyone stop him. He was not happy with where he was at the time in life and didn't know how to juggle all of the mixed emotions that came along with it.

He expressed that he felt really bad, especially after he had received my poem. He was a little shocked after receiving it because he had never heard me express my feelings in that type of way towards him. He admitted to being selfish and believes he could've said something. But he had previously tried the serious relationship thing with the ex. At one point, he had thought she could've been the one. But the effort he was putting into the relationship was draining, and it pulled him away from his goals. All they did was argue. He felt that having a good woman by your side should make you a better man, not bring you down. He had opened up to her and spoiled her with lots of gifts and trips etc., all to not end up together." So, then I told myself, maybe relationships aren't my thing", he said to me.

"But I could not shake you out of my head," he also said. He mentioned how he tried to casually date just to have fun for the moment. That's exactly all it was, for the moment, because no one gave him that feeling to take anything further. He explained to me that when a man is not where he wants to be in life, it's very difficult for him to commit to anyone. It was challenging for him because he knew he felt something for me, but he was too deep in his own head to follow those feelings. He then told me that he still follows me on social media and again expressed how proud of me he was and how some of my posts have gotten him through a lot of challenging situations.

He consistently apologized and told me he wanted to make things right. Hearing those words felt like a weight had been lifted off my shoulders. I couldn't believe that after all this time, not a single feeling towards this man had left. That's how I knew I was still in love. The old me probably would've questioned my worth or lowered my standards for someone else and settled just to say I have someone. But I stayed true to myself and kept my faith in God that one day I would be appreciated and loved by the right one. Until then, I am focused on myself.

I didn't give in that easily to Darren that night at dinner. Granted, I missed him and wanted to be with him, but I was previously hurt, and it took a lot to overcome that. I never wanted to experience that pain again. My soul could not handle another broken bond, especially with the wrong person. I made it clear to him that I didn't want anything other than natural, pure, and genuine energy in my life right now. I had no time for any mixed emotions or confusion.

We began to take things slow. We never went over to each other's homes, and sex was not a thing. We'd always meet in public places; sometimes, I'd have my son. We had to try to "learn each other" all over again. I treated him accordingly. He put forth a lot of effort; he was persistent. We went on dates, worked out together, text consistently throughout the day while working; he even started coming to church with me. That was major! Whenever I wasn't speaking to the youth, we would go to the main sanctuary on Sundays. He understood my walk with God and that I was determined to go wherever he was leading me. I wanted nothing but what God had in store for me and my child.

After a few months, we began to question what it was that we were doing. Was it a "courting thing"? Are we just going with the flow? Is this some type of trial period, or what? He mentioned previously how he had started cooking more during our time apart. He insisted that he cooked for me. He asked if I would come over at the end of the week. I tried to make arrangements, but I had absolutely no one to keep my son. After explaining that I couldn't make it, he said, "It's FINE, Teyanna, bring my boy." I agreed, and we went.

It felt so good being in his house with my son. He was much older now at this point, still active but well-behaved. He spent most of his time on Darren's tablet after we ate. Even while we ate, he was not worried about us; he was focused on the games. This was the night we made it official; we became boyfriend and girlfriend. I cannot remember the last time I was anyone's girlfriend. I dated periodically, but a relationship? It had to be well over ten years. Does that even count?

Gradually, we became acquainted with each other's family. His parents weren't together, but they both were a part of his life. He had a great relationship with each of them. I went to family cookouts, his mom styled my hair; she was a beautician, and I went fishing with him and his dad. I even went to his grandma's house for Sunday dinner. I was well-known on his end.

When it came to my family, my dad was still not around. By this time in my life, we had gotten in touch with one another, but he was still inconsistent, just like in my younger days. My brother accepted him, and they pretty much clicked immediately. My mom was pretty tough on him and drilled him down every chance she got. It was a little too much at times, but I knew she had my best interest at heart. Her main concern was me becoming a single mother of two. I hate that she even put that thought in the atmosphere, but I get it now.

Things weren't always "peaches and cream" with us. We had disagreements here and there, but he never disrespected me, he never put his hands on me, and he remained committed to me. The behavior was mutual, and I knew that regardless of any disagreement, I didn't want anyone else other than him. We remained in separate homes, which became challenging at times because I had a mortgage, and his lease wasn't up anytime soon during that period. But it did give us a chance to miss one another.

Darren was still ambitious, and stagnation was a huge turn-off for him. He consistently asked about my plans for my business idea, and I kept mentioning them. It was a Non-Profit organization. I kept explaining to him that it takes money to make money. I wasn't broke, but I wasn't financially set in a position to invest money from my bill funds. He sat down with me and introduced me to so much new information and resources. He gave me a list of grants to apply for. He helped me write out a business plan and apply for credit cards; the whole nine, he took the initiative and led me.

The more I learned from him, the more excited I became. The more approvals I got, the more I knew it was getting serious. It was getting serious with becoming a business owner and even more serious with the two of us. He was so serious that once his lease was up, he moved in with us. Things were different, and it took a lot for my son to adjust. Slowly but surely, he got used to it. I was so happy in life. Things had finally started working out for me. At times, I'd pinch myself to see if I was actually dreaming.

Never have I ever experienced a full household with two adults who loved each other, paid bills, and raised a child together. That's right, he stepped up a lot. This wasn't even something I asked him to do. He just naturally took on tasks and insisted on taking some weight off my shoulders. Why not, though? Albert was still not around.

We'd decided to host Thanksgiving at our place that year. His parents, a few siblings, my mom and brother, aunts, and a few of his friends were over. It was so much fun! We ate well, played lots of games, talked a lot of junk over the card table, and watched the kids play in the backyard. Before everyone left, each of us began taking turns explaining what we were thankful for. When it was my turn, I thanked everyone for the experience and explained that the joy that I felt was indescribable. It felt amazing being surrounded by love in my own place with my son and my man. I couldn't have asked for a better Thanksgiving. We continued taking turns, letting everyone speak.

When it was Darren's turn, he began by thanking everyone for coming out to spend the holiday with us. Those who traveled far and those who lived close. He then looked at my son and thanked him personally for allowing him into his home and sharing his mom. I thought that was the funniest thing ever. My baby pulled his shades down like he was top-flight security and dapped him up. Afterward, he looks at me, smiling from ear to ear.

I remember his exact words as he grabbed both my hands; "But you, Teyanna. I'm thankful to you for not giving up on me. Even when things didn't go as planned, you didn't give up. Yes, you focused on your dreams, and we went our separate ways. But you never stopped praying. I believe that because I know it was no one but God that brought us back together. I knew when I first laid eyes on you that you were the one. Everything was so natural, and nothing was ever forced between us. I now understand that everything happens for a reason and that there's a time for everything. Which is why I want to tell you in front of everyone that I love you so much, and I love the way that you love me. I love everything about you. You match me, you inspire me, and you've made me into a better man."

He then let go of my hands and got on one knee. My heart was beating so fast; I was trying so hard not to cry if only I could show a picture of my facial expression, smiling and holding back tears. Once I heard those words, "Teyanna, will you marry me?" The tears came down. I couldn't speak. I screamed so loud, "Yes, yes"! He stood up and hugged me so tight. I never wanted him to let me go. He whispered in my ear, "I love you, girl." I then wiped my tears and turned to look for my son. He was struggling, holding about three dozen red roses and a balloon. I picked him up and kissed his cheek. I began to cry again, "We're getting married!" I yelled. I didn't think my day could get any better. But this topped it off, especially my ring!

As everyone began to leave, my cousin suggested my son stay over at her house to play with her son. That was the best idea ever. Because that night, we made love like no other. I was woken up the next morning to a beautiful breakfast in bed. I could tell a lot of thought and effort was put into it by the presentation. I smiled, but I didn't seem too "excited". The truth is, I had come back to realization and realized that I shouldn't have done what I did the previous night. As tempting as it was and as deeply in love as I was with him, I should have set boundaries. Here I am, now a woman of God, having sexual relations prior to the two of us becoming one flesh.

Yes, I had sinned in the past. But those sins had been forgiven. Just like this one, I had to repent. I explained to Darren that it wasn't right. If he really loved me and followed the same God, he would wait. We prayed and let it go. I had never in my life prayed with a man. Not even my own father. This was amazing! I just could not believe this was happening. After everything I had been through, I never imagined this. It was almost too good to be true.

TWELVE

Power

Over time, roughly about a month or two, I was still on cloud nine from the engagement. I worked from home, but every chance I got, I was showing off my ring on camera. Of course, I posted it on social media, and my notifications went crazy! I was overwhelmed with joy. We began planning immediately. Not a day went by that I wasn't thinking about the ceremony. We picked the summer of the following year, three weeks after his birthday.

    In the meantime, we continued living our happy lives, going to work, parenting, going on family outings, and even going on dates together. I told Darren that my mind was back heavy on the Non-Profit. I would dream about it and wake up thinking about it. We then filed all the necessary documents after creating my name. A month later, the official document had come in the mail. What an extreme of happiness that caused!

It was official; legally, I had a non-profit organization. But it was just me; who else was going to be a part of the organization? I then got someone to create me a flyer to post about an interest meeting. It was for single moms. Granted, not everyone is a single mom, and I wanted the organization to be built by women like me who had experienced similar situations so that they could empathize with the ones we'd be helping in the near future.

The turnout was more than I expected. Yes, I had created a huge fan base, but I did not know that so many other moms were interested in helping single moms. Alice and I were back consistently speaking. Of course, she was a part of the group. One thing she's going to do is support me in whatever I do. I genuinely appreciated her. She was my personal assistant and right hand through it all. The organization took off! We hosted lots of fundraisers and received lots of donations.

We'd get a lot of reposts on social media, which meant our name was spreading. It was great. It wasn't a smooth process all the time. We struggled periodically in the beginning because we were using our own money. The ladies paid monthly dues, and Alice and I picked up the backend. We did what we could, but we never lost our faith.

We had dedicated members for quite some time. But then, like dominoes, they started slacking and not taking it as seriously as expected. Some started missing a lot of meetings, not paying dues, and then created drama within. It began to get smaller and smaller. I became so frustrated and slightly overwhelmed. So overwhelmed to the point that I made myself sick.

I was sick for weeks, vomiting, headaches, cramping, and just so irritated. I thought I had driven myself crazy. I thought I had driven myself crazy until my cycle was late. Almost an entire month had gone by, and it still had not come. I didn't understand because it had just previously come the past month, so it couldn't have been a pregnancy. I made myself a doctor's appointment just for peace of mind. That's exactly what I had received, a PIECE of mind. Because the other portion of it was being used for the development of a seed, yes, another baby was growing in my womb. Turns out I did not have an actual period that last month. It was implantation bleeding.

    My excitement was indescribable. I was in shock because being pregnant was the last thing on my mind. However, I'm engaged and actually with someone who really loves me this time. I couldn't wait to tell him. I have such a creative mindset; I did not want to be simple when breaking the news. I had to think of something special. I told him I wanted to take a break from the organization for a while so that I could create a plan to become bigger. In the meantime, I was just going to practice self-care and focus on the wedding.

The truth is, I was waiting until Valentine's Day to surprise him. It was so hard not to share with him my every thought about the pregnancy. I held it in until the next month. I began giving him clues every other day and told him this Valentine's Day was going to be like no other. Once the day had come, he had already made reservations for us downtown on a rooftop. We had a really great time; there was a beautiful ambiance, great service, and amazing food. While waiting for the check, I pulled out a gift box from my large purse.

It was a small, red, square-shaped, flat box. I handed it to him while saying, "Happy Valentine's

Day, baby." He smiled while taking it. As he opened it, he said, "What are you up to now?" It was a baby onesie that read "My first Valentine ."His brows wrinkled. He had a look of confusion. Then, he opened a black envelope with a white card and red writing that read, "Roses are red, Violets are blue, on your birthday I am due." "WHATTTTTT?!" He yelled while smiling and looking like he wanted to cry. He then kissed me and said, "We're about to have a baby." He was so happy! I was speechless. All I could do was laugh and cry at the same time. My hormones were already all over the place.

    The wedding had to be pushed back because we picked a date three weeks after his birthday. But the baby was due on his actual birthday. No way was I walking down the aisle three weeks prior to dropping a baby. We had to notify all our guests and vendors. It was literally seven months away by this time.

I knew that Darren was going to be a great father. He was already a good father figure to my son, who was also excited about becoming a big brother. He's so sweet. Throughout the pregnancy, he was amazing. What a complete opposite of my first. I did not want for anything. Whatever I wanted, whatever I needed, he was there. No matter what it was, foot rubs, quiet time, help bathing, a snack in the middle of the night, carrying objects, you name it, he did it. He even reminded me that I was beautiful, even if I felt huge. He never missed a doctor's appointment, and he always took time to talk to my stomach. He was determined that the baby came out already knowing who he was.

Months had gone by, and we were almost at the finish line. I had gotten bigger, and he had gotten more excited. It was the final month; I had four more weeks to go. As we prepared for the shower, my mind began to have flashbacks of the first baby shower. I remembered how frustrating it was for me to do everything on my own with the help of my mom. This time was different, very different. Darren was a workaholic and determined to succeed, so he worked every opportunity he had. Especially now that we were bringing a newborn into this world, he wanted to be sure we wanted for nothing, and that's exactly what happened. He wasn't really into all the planning and prepping; instead, he just sent the funds and asked me to let him know what I decided to do.

It was beautiful! Everything was color coordinated, the food was good, but the vibes were even better. We received lots of gifts and words of encouragement. I danced so much that he had to help me get in the tub to soak at the end of the night. I must have forgotten that dancing led my first one out. I was supposed to be waiting at least three more weeks by this time. I guess God had other plans because I tossed and turned all night to the point where I was gripping his arms due to the pain and pressure I was feeling.

I began to count the time in between the contractions; they were not far apart from one another. It was time; the baby was on the way. Our bags were already packed and downstairs near the door. He got my son dressed and then put him in the car. He then helped me downstairs, put my shoes on my feet, and helped me get in as well. I screamed and turned the entire ride. While en route, I asked him to call my mom. I couldn't do this without her there. I also wanted someone to watch my son while Darren assisted me.

By the time we got to the hospital, I was already at/around 8cm. Once we got the medicine in my system, within an hour, I was at 10cm, and it was time to push. My mother had arrived by this time. I had her, my son, and Darren there for support. I didn't want my baby to see my insides, especially at his age, and look the way it looked. I didn't know that my mom had contacted nearly the whole family, as well as Darren's. So, he ended up waiting in the lobby with everyone else.

I was as numb as I could get. I felt absolutely nothing. I had Darren on one side and the nurse on the other. My mom was recording. "Push, Push, Push!" the midwife yelled. As I squeezed his hand, I could feel the sweat from his nervousness. But it didn't stop him from encouraging me to keep pushing while telling me how beautiful I was and how much he loved me. I couldn't react the way I wanted to, but hearing those words made my heart melt. I needed to hear it because it encouraged me to keep trying and made me more excited to see what we had created.

Just like that, he slid out of the birth canal and cried his little heart out. That's right; "he". I had given birth to another son, Darren Jr. I couldn't have been prouder. He was perfect. Everything was just as I imagined, the ones who loved me the most surrounded me and my beautiful, healthy baby boy. Once they took the baby to get a bath, the gifts and flowers started rolling in. I felt so blessed and beyond thankful for the kind words and arrangements.

But wait, it gets better; my man handed me a huge vase of red roses with a card attached. The card felt weird because it wasn't flat. It was something rocky inside. It was a key, along with a small piece of paper with an address on it. I was so confused. "What's this for"? I asked. "It's for your new event space," he said. "For your organization and events that you throw. You don't have to rent out buildings or meet in public locations anymore," he also added.

Tears began falling down my face; I was speechless. I couldn't do anything but cry and try to smile behind all the sniffing. He then leaned in to hug me, "Oh my Gosh, thank you." "Thank you. I love you so much", I said to him. No man had ever done anything like that for me before. I barely got a box of chocolate. That was the best push gift ever. I didn't even know he knew about push gifts.

After a few days, they let us go home. Darren did the best he could to try and get the hang of the newborn phase. He had never really interacted with one this closely before. I taught him as much as I could, and it was easy doing so because he listened. I could tell he was excited and very much determined to be the best father he could be. He constantly reminded me that I didn't have to do certain things because he knew how I did it all on my own for years with my first. I made it very clear to him when we got together that I never wanted to experience anything like that again.

    To this day, he's such an amazing father. The wedding ended up being ten months after the baby had arrived. We didn't want to wait any longer. We ended up using our building to host our reception. Finally, we were officially legal. Things weren't always smooth every day. But we loved each other enough to work through it. Although we didn't always see eye to eye, there were never any severe arguments about things that could lead to us departing ways.

    We were still actively involved with the church. I still spoke on every third Sunday, and we still went to bible study together throughout the week. Never did I imagine that I would become a youth minister and get married with two kids. I always saw myself as a rich TV presenter or an actress. But God had different plans for me.

It was very boring and somewhat difficult at first being single and celibate for so long. It was quite a challenge not to settle at first. It took lots and lots of discipline. For years, I hadn't gone on dates, and no one was kissing me, touching me, admiring me, or just having fun with me. It was always just me and my son. I thought I would be struggling forever to raise this kid on my own while trying to do whatever I could to bring in money to provide.

But God chose me. He could've chosen anyone else. Instead, he chose me and made me uncomfortable with my old ways. He had already ordered my steps, meaning no matter which way I tried to run, I would still end up exactly where he wanted me to be. I knew I had a purpose and that he loved me a long time ago. I was just somewhat nervous about what people would think if I stepped into my calling. Then I realized these people can't judge me. If they knew better, they'd do better. If only they knew that when you sacrifice something for him, and when you're obedient and follow his orders, he will come through for you.

He will place you above all those who tried to pray against and sabotage you. All those people who intentionally did you wrong and mistreated you. He'll have your back; they will be punished and falling at your feet. But you will be blessed beyond what you can imagine. Indeed, I was blessed. I had a good God-fearing man who loved me for me and loved my son as his own. He loved my son so much that he legally adopted him. I was no longer concerned about Albert and if he would ever come around.

My son was six years old, and we still had not heard from him. My God has that entire situation under control. What some people don't realize is that you reap what you sew. He gave us these children; the children did not send a special request to be here. When you don't take care of these precious babies, he will not take care of you. You may wonder why things are not going accordingly and why you feel somewhat cursed. Because you are not being obedient, nor are you fully committed to him.

Just as we commit to those people who are no good for us, the ones who are not intended to go to the next level. We should commit to God. You have no idea what he has in store for you if you just trust him. I have a job that I enjoy, that allows me to balance my personal life along with my work life. My business is prospering, my husband's business is prospering, and our kids are healthy and in need of nothing. Mentally, I am free; spiritually, I am free; emotionally, I am free. I am free from all the heartache, free from pain, free from abandonment, free from depression, free from negativity.

I am really proud of the woman I have become, and I can't do anything but give all glory to God. My mindset has changed tremendously, the way I speak and the way I carry myself; I have, and I am still evolving. I love this new version of me. I chose myself and did what was best for me so that I could learn to be the best version of myself for my child. Some individuals in life have given up on themselves. But I learned that I, in particular, had been blessed with the courage to get ready for the next level. When I decided that enough was enough and realized I had nowhere else to run, I knew who to call on. Everything I thought I had lost was given back to me times ten.

So, when you find yourself in situations that seem uncomfortable and toxic when you notice things aren't going as smoothly as you intended for them to go, take some time to pray and ask him to reveal what it is that he's trying to tell you. Everything happens for a reason; you just have to listen. What's meant to be will be. When things don't work out, look at it like it's not a part of the plan, or maybe this is not the right time. You might be delayed a blessing because you're still holding onto something or someone that God has no desire to bless. Love yourself first before you try to love anyone else. Once you create that positive version of yourself, you can finally be capable of loving others versus hurting them, including your children.

Let go of what your ex did, your parents, relatives, and so-called friends. Forgive them, even if they never apologize. Holding on to that anger and pain will do absolutely nothing but bring you down while impacting your health negatively. I never forgave and went back to those relationships or environments. I simply forgave myself for my sanity and to create my own happiness.

Lastly, remember that everyone is not intended to go to the next level with you. It could be your family or even a friend. Anything that is meant to be will not have to be forced. Don't make regretful decisions based on emotions; before you do anything, pray about it. Seek Godly relationships and surround yourself with the ones who make you feel loved, safe, and at peace; it's good for your soul. Take back your POWER!

ABOUT THE AUTHOR

Tabitha C. is a self-published author from Atlanta, GA. She started writing at the young age of 25 and published her first book a few years later. Tabitha's favorite writing technique is narrating; she is very fond of telling stories, whether they're based on a true event or made up. She enjoys adding details to her writing and forcing readers to create a visual image of the story. Tabitha's novels are based on situations she has either experienced personally or witnessed by others. In this particular story, she took the input of other single moms and transformed their personal stories into one single character. Tabitha believes that all women are different but still similar in various ways. She believes that life can be viewed from different angles, but there is only one creator, and with him, all things are possible.

Made in the USA
Columbia, SC
29 March 2024

33799748R00120